THE INVITATION

A PSYCHOLOGICAL SUSPENSE THRILLER

N. L. HINKENS

Published by Dunecadia Publishing, California

ISBN: 978-1-947890-38-1

Cover by: **www.derangeddoctordesign.com**

Editing by: **www.jeanette-morris.com/first-impressions-writing**

1

Angela Marshall had resorted to walking her dog as soon as it was light out every morning. Between the never-ending swarm of mindless tourists buzzing around the shore of Tamarack Creek Lake, and the growing hordes of second-home urbanites with their inflatable neon flamingos and noxious jet boats, the once undiscovered gem, was now virtually unrecognizable. Dawn had become her favorite time of day to view the lake, like liquid silver before the wind kicked up, undisturbed by the recreational boaters and their infernal speakers polluting the deep peace afforded only by nature. Apart from the slow, successive chirping of the osprey over-head, or the occasional lone fish performing a spectacular flip for an audience of two, she and her aging black Lab, Duke, had the lake to themselves.

"Ugh," she grunted as she bent over to unclip his leash, her inflamed knuckles not cooperating with her brain. Arthritis was winning the battle, her grip weakening by the day. It wouldn't be long before she was denied even the simple pleasure of taking Duke for his daily walk. Age was a tyrant that granted no mercy. Her husband, Ronnie, had gone from a brilliant neurologist to a gibbering shell of a man in a three-month period before he'd passed away last fall. Duke was the reason she'd been able to keep going. He needed her as much as she needed him.

A relieved sigh slipped through her lips when the leash finally came free. She rummaged around in her coat pocket for a rubber ball and flung it as far as she could down the sandy shore. "Fetch, boy!"

Chuckling to herself, she watched as Duke bolted over the sand—his aging hips momentarily forgotten—racing against himself to retrieve his favorite toy. She waited for him to snatch it up and bring it back to her, but when he reached the water's edge, he lost interest in his mission and took a hard left instead. Nose down, he began investigating a more intriguing scent in the submerged pondweed.

"Oh, no!" Angela groused as she watched him splash his way into the water. The last thing she wanted to do this morning was wrestle a decaying fish from his jaws. Like every other canine, he seemed to be morbidly fixated on dead things.

Grimacing, she shuffled down the sandy shore, almost tripping on a half-buried piece of driftwood in her path. Chiding herself to be more careful, she trudged onward. Only last week, her friend Dot had tripped over a hose in her yard and lain in the dirt for over two hours with a broken hip before a UPS driver had discovered her.

As Angela drew closer to the water's edge, Duke began barking frantically, alternately sniffing at the weeds and backing away. She tried calling him to heel, but he paid her no mind. When she finally reached the shoreline, she was forced to wade ankle deep into the lake to get a hold of his collar. After struggling for a minute or two, she managed to latch the leash, but he continued to whine and tug toward whatever was in the weeds.

Careful not to lose her balance in her slippery tennis shoes, she squinted into the murky depths to see what had caught his attention. Her eyesight had deteriorated of late, and it was hard to see much without her glasses. She was scheduled for cataract surgery next week, which meant having to stay with her overbearing sister for a few days. She'd only consented to the surgery because her doctor had assured her it would give her vision a new lease on life. Pity he couldn't do something about the arthritis while he was at it.

Turning to go, she spotted several white sticks intertwined with the curly green fronds of pondweed bobbing just below the surface of the water. Her heart shuddered. The branch they were connected to looked almost like ... an arm. *No!* It couldn't be. She must be seeing things. Blinking, she took a hesitant step forward and peered more closely into the tangled weeds. Her eyes widened in horror as several dark, trailing strands of hair parted to reveal a chalky face.

A blood-curdling scream hurtled its way up her throat, shattering the peace of the morning.

2

ONE DAY EARLIER

"Alex! Bring the rest of the groceries in from the car!" Maria called to her husband as she began transferring the cold items from the cooler into the refrigerator. Glancing out the panoramic kitchen window of her lake house, she gazed at the soft, white, corrugated waves lapping their way toward shore. The wooden dock see-sawed slowly back-and-forth, the aluminum boat tied to it gently nudging its bumper as it bobbed. She could stare at the lake for hours. The many moods of the water had always fascinated her—there was something distinctly womanly about its complexity.

Rolling her aching shoulders, she reached for a gallon of milk. It always felt like she was going down a gear when she came up to the lake—a welcome break from the hectic pace of her life, especially of late. Admittedly, it was a bit of a hassle lugging groceries and coolers, but it was always worth the effort. There was nothing she enjoyed more than sitting out on the back deck in the morning watching ducks dive-bombing for breakfast beneath the shimmering surface of the water. The serenity of the place alone was enough to counteract all the stress of running her company. Not that she was complaining.

XCellNourish had taken off in a big way this year—which is what they were there to celebrate this weekend.

She'd invited her two senior managers, Ricki and Ivy, along with their spouses, to join her and Alex—a reward of sorts for hitting all their sales goals, and then some. She couldn't have accomplished it without Ricki and Ivy on board. They were both rock solid assets. They'd worked hard alongside her every step of the way to take the business to the top of its game, and they deserved to be acknowledged for the crucial role they'd played in her success. In her wildest dreams, she would never have guessed nutritional supplements would be so lucrative.

Maria frowned as she put the cooler away. She would have to remind Alex not to start bragging about the twins this weekend. Their boys were both at college studying law, and Alex liked nothing more than to sing their praises. In light of the fact that Ivy and Jim had recently lost their only daughter, and Ricki and Brock were unable to have children, the twins were a topic best steered clear of if she wanted to keep the mood light.

She glanced up as Alex strode into the kitchen and plonked the remaining bags of groceries onto the counter. "Want these unpacked?" he asked, his tone decidedly grumpy.

Maria shook her head. "No. You'll just put things in strange places and then I'll waste time looking for them. Why don't you set up the patio instead? Get out the cushions and citronella candles. We're having steak tonight, so make sure the grill's clean."

"Yes ma'am," Alex replied with a stiff salute, before heading out to the deck.

Maria sighed as she watched him beat a hasty retreat. It always took her a few hours to switch hats from CEO to weekender. Alex didn't get it. He couldn't relate to the pressure she was under. As a freelance writer, he set his own pace and hours, while she was beholden to customers and deadlines—all the while juggling production issues, shipping calamities, and finances, not to mention the headache of dealing with forty-two employees. It had been weeks since she had made it up to the lake house to enjoy a few days off. Alex wasn't the most supportive spouse. He seemed to resent her growing success. At least, that's what she attributed his dour attitude of late too. It didn't help that he wasn't making much progress on his latest novel. She'd snuck a look at his manuscript last week and been shocked to discover that he'd only written two pages in the past month. What on earth was he doing with all the time he spent at the lake house alone?

After preparing a marinade for the steaks, she headed upstairs to unpack her bag. She carried her toiletries into the bathroom and took a few minutes to freshen up. She was looking forward to spending some unscheduled time with Ricki and Ivy and letting her hair down a little. Alex could make some of his famous margaritas, and they could hang out on the deck and watch the sunset while they ate. No reservations, no fighting traffic in the city to get to some crowded, overpriced restaurant. Pure bliss.

She zipped up her make up bag and shoved it into the cabinet beneath the sink, knocking over Alex's leather toiletry bag in the process. As she hurriedly scooped the contents back inside, she noticed something bulging in the inner zippered pocket. Opening it, she discovered a prescription bottle with a missing label. She tipped some of the pills into the palm of her hand and studied them. Were they prescription pills? They were stamped, but she couldn't read the letters without her glasses, which she'd left downstairs. They certainly weren't from the *XCellNourish* supplement line.

Baffled, she slipped one of the pills into the pocket of her hoodie to ask Alex about later and made her way back downstairs. She would wait until he was done setting up the patio. It was never a good idea to interrupt him when he was on task. It was next to impossible to get him to focus on anything for longer than a few minutes. At the rate he was going, he would never finish his novel—another topic best avoided if she wanted to keep the peace this weekend.

For the next half hour or so, she bustled about dusting surfaces and plumping up the cushions on the couch. She set out a few candles and retrieved the margarita glasses from the cupboard. It had been a while since they'd enjoyed a couples' weekend at the lake.

Hopefully, Alex would be on his best behavior. He had as many moods as the lake itself sometimes.

"I swept off the patio and cleaned the BBQ," he said, striding back into the kitchen. He tugged a hand through his hair, glancing distractedly around the space. "Are we done now?"

"Almost. Can you check the guest bedrooms and make sure the beds are made up and ready to go with fresh towels?" Maria bit her lip and frowned as she pulled out the small oval pill she'd stashed in her pocket. "I found these pills in your shaving bag. What are they?"

Alex shot her a look of alarm. "Uh, just some antidepressants."

Maria gaped at him in disbelief. They'd been married for twenty-eight years, and he'd never mentioned being depressed before. Granted, he could be moody at times, but weren't all writers that way? "What are you doing with antidepressants?"

Alex narrowed his eyes. "What do you think I'm doing with them?"

Maria inhaled a quick, calming breath before answering. The last thing she wanted to do was start a fight before the other couples arrived. Ricki and Ivy were intuitive enough to sniff out the remnants of an argument lingering in the atmosphere in half a heartbeat. She tried a different tack. "How long have you been taking them?"

"I dunno. Couple of months."

Maria twisted the pill between her thumb and forefinger. "I don't understand. The company's doing great. For the first time in years, we don't have to worry about money. Why are you feeling depressed now, all of a sudden? Are you sick or something?"

Alex shrugged, averting his eyes. "No particular reason. The doctor says it's not uncommon for men my age. Just a rough patch. My writing's stalled of late." He folded his arms defensively across his chest. "As you've been quick to point out."

"That's not fair, Alex. I only ask about your writing because I care," Maria responded, trying to sound more supportive than accusatory. "Why didn't you talk to me about this?"

Alex blinked at her, struggling to come up with a response.

"You've ... had a lot on your plate. It wasn't worth bothering you about. It's no big deal."

"It *is* a big deal! I'd like to know if my husband is feeling depressed enough to see a doctor and get a prescription."

The expression on Alex's face hardened. "You mean it's a big deal if the husband of *XCellNourish's* CEO is taking prescription pills instead of touting some homeopathic concoction to fix his brain."

Maria clenched a fist at her side. This was exactly the lane she didn't want to be in right now. Her business had become an increasingly touchy subject as profits soared. She couldn't really blame Alex for trying to hide the fact from her that he was taking antidepressants. It wasn't good advertising for a company whose slogan was *Natural is Best*. She had little choice but to drop the subject for now. Their guests were due to show up at any minute. But she wasn't finished with the topic. Alex hadn't come clean about why he was feeling depressed. He was lying about the pills. And she intended to find out why.

3

"Hurry up, Brock!" Ricki called, as she slid behind the wheel of her BMW coupe. "We need to get on the road if we're going to make it to the lake before dinner."

"Yes, I know. You've told me that five times already!" Brock grumbled, as he strode over to the car. "Did you grab my bag?"

Ricki gave a terse nod. "Right there on the back seat."

Brock glanced over his shoulder at it before climbing in. "I still don't understand why I have to come with you this weekend," he huffed, adjusting his seatbelt as she pulled out onto the street. "We just had dinner with Maria and Alex last month."

Ricki shot him a steely look. "I told you why. We've had our most successful quarter to date, and Maria wants to celebrate with her managers and their spouses—at her lake house, no less. What's so bad about that?"

"Nothing," Brock replied, staring sullenly through the windshield.

"This is about our future," Ricki continued. "Maria offered me a stock option bonus this year. Do you have any idea what that might mean for us down the line? Besides, it's not as if you had anything else going on this weekend."

"I had plans to go golfing with Dave."

Ricki jerked her head in his direction at the mention of golf. The knot in her stomach tightened. "Again? You just went last weekend."

"So? You'd go shopping every weekend if you could," Brock retorted. "I don't know why you jump down my throat every time I bring up golf. You're the one who told me to get a hobby."

Tamping down her anger, Ricki stared fixedly ahead as she sped along the highway. He must think she was stupid. She knew full well why he'd been avoiding her of late. He'd never been a fan of golf, but now, all of a sudden, he was a fanatic—grabbing every opportunity to disappear for hours at a time on the weekend. She could no longer deny the glaring reality that their relationship was fraying at the edges. Her recent promotion to VP of Marketing meant she was rarely home at night before seven-thirty or eight. They used to have a routine of cooking dinner together in the evenings. Brock would pour them each a glass of wine while he prepped the vegetables and they filled each other in on their respective days.

Nowadays, it was more a case of dumping a few cartons of Chinese takeout onto paper plates and reheating it. By the time she got through eating, she was too tired to talk, and Brock was engrossed in his latest episodic survival show. A couple of times, he'd even gone out for drinks after work with a colleague—something he never used to do mid-week. She'd accused him of doing it just to punish her for coming home late, and they'd had a huge argument about it. Afterward, she'd regretted some of the things she'd said and apologized. But things had been strained between them since.

"What does Maria's husband do again?" Brock asked, sending her dark thoughts skittering back to the shadowy crevices of her brain.

"He's an author."

"In other words, nothing," Brock muttered, twisting his lips in disapproval.

Ricki seethed inwardly. Lately, Brock seemed to be hung up on money. He'd become overly sensitive to the earning potential of everyone in their social circle—herself included. Before *XCellNourish* had become profitable, he'd been the primary breadwinner as a moderately successful civil engineer. This year, she'd eclipsed his paycheck by several celestial zeros, and this is where it had got her. Her marriage was in shambles. "Look, if you're going to be like this all weekend, you might as well not come," Ricki admonished him. "You could at least make an effort to be sociable."

"I am. That's why I'm asking. But I still wish Maria had made it a girls' weekend and left us guys out of the mix."

Ricki grimaced. If she could have gotten out of this weekend herself, she would have, but she wasn't about to admit that to Brock. "I guess you'll just have to suck it up then, won't you?"

"Sounds like we're in for a great time," Brock said dryly, as she pulled off the highway and turned onto the road leading to Tamarack Creek Lake.

Ricki bit back a stinging retort. It was pointless bickering back-and-forth like this. Her stomach was already a cesspool of acid. They would be pulling up outside Maria's lake house any minute now, and she didn't want to climb out of the car with a frozen smile on her face that her eagle-eyed boss would see straight through. She knew how much Maria had been anticipating this weekend, so she couldn't ruin it for her. Maria had mentioned more than once how good it would be for Alex to have the guys up to the lake house. She blamed the fact that he didn't seem to have any real friends on the harsh reality that writing was an isolating occupation. But as Ivy had pointed out to Ricki, scuba diving was an isolating occupation too, and her husband, Jim, a commercial diver, had no shortage of friends. Ivy and Ricki had become close during the time they'd worked together at *XCellNourish*. Their bond had only strengthened since Ivy's daughter's untimely death a few months earlier. Ricki shuddered at the memory of that awful time. She couldn't imagine losing a child in such a tragic manner. Miscarrying was painful enough.

"Is this where we turn?" Brock asked, interrupting her thoughts.

Ricki glanced at the GPS on her phone. "Yes. Maria said to go past the A-frame log cabin set back from the road on the left and then it's the next house after that."

Moments later, they turned onto a gravel driveway and parked behind a black Audi.

"Only one vehicle," Brock noted, as she turned off the ignition. "Jim and Ivy must not be here yet."

"Ivy said they might be a little late. They had to drop their cat off at her mom's." Ricki flipped down the sunshade and checked her make up in the mirror, before applying a slick of nude lip gloss. Her complexion was pale beneath her foundation and her eyes signaled a troubled spirit. She would need to toughen up and mask her unhappiness before she went inside.

Brock climbed out and grabbed both their bags from the back seat. Ricki reached for her purse and flashed him a stilted smile—silently begging him to keep up the appearance of a happy marriage for the next forty-eight hours.

"Hey guys! Welcome to the lake!" Maria called from the front steps.

Ricki waved back, forcing herself to smile as she greeted her boss.

"I'm so glad you're here," Maria gushed, hugging her tightly. "We're going to have a blast this weekend. If the weather's nice, we'll take the boat out tomorrow."

Brock walked up behind them holding a bag in each hand. He glanced around admiringly. "Your place is incredible."

"Thanks, we love coming up here. It's so peaceful," Maria replied, beaming at him. "I'll show you guys your room so you can get situated before dinner. I sent Alex down to the shed to fetch some wood for the fire pit. It's a beautiful evening, so I thought we could eat outside and enjoy the sunset later."

As she turned to lead them upstairs, Alex appeared in the doorway, brushing wood chips from his clothes.

"Ah, here he is now!" Maria cried. "Just in time to make us some of his famous margaritas. Jack-of-all-trades, aren't you, honey?"

He shot her a frosty look before nodding a greeting to Ricki and Brock.

Ricki grinned back uneasily. Apparently, they weren't the only couple teetering on the edge of war before the weekend had even begun.

4

"Wow! Check out that view of the lake!" Jim exclaimed, as they turned into Maria's driveway. "It looks stunning with the mountains in the backdrop!"

"It sure is," Ivy replied. "It's crazy there's still snow on the peaks in July."

Jim pulled in behind the other cars and turned off the engine.

"If you park here, you'll be blocking everyone in," Ivy pointed out.

Jim grunted. "Won't matter. We're not going anywhere for the next two days."

"Isn't their house beautiful?" Ivy observed, as they made their way up the steps to the front door. "I love all the stone cladding."

"A custom home like this doesn't come cheap," Jim commented.

Ivy nodded, her eyes feasting on the exquisite exterior and manicured lawn sweeping down to the beach. She could only ever dream of living in a place like this. But maybe the stock option Maria had promised her would make that dream a reality someday soon if *XCell-Nourish* continued on the course it was on.

"Knock, knock. Anyone home?" she called through the open doorway.

"Yay! You're here!" Maria answered, as she came running out to greet them. "Perfect timing. We were just about to have a cocktail. Alex made a bucketload of margaritas to get the party started. Ricki and Brock are already here. You can drop your bags by the stairs, for now, if you want. I'll show you your room later."

Ivy shot a warning look Jim's way, but he purposely avoided looking at her. The only cloud hanging over this weekend was her fear that Jim would drink too much and make an idiot of himself. He'd developed a bit of a drinking problem after their daughter's tragic death. He didn't consider it a problem, but he wasn't fooling Ivy. She knew all about the empty bottles he tried to hide at the bottom of the trash can. He resented the fact that she had *moved on* as he called it—which was nonsense, of course. She could never move on from losing her only child, but she'd managed to pick up the pieces of her shattered life and throw herself back into work after taking a few weeks off to grieve. She'd even signed up for painting classes—something she'd always wanted to do but never gotten around to. She wasn't naive enough to think she would ever paint a masterpiece, but she found it therapeutic. Emily would have wanted her to keep on growing, and exploring, and enjoying life.

Jim, on the other hand, seemed bent on endlessly churning his wheels in a rut of grief. At first, he'd been consumed by rage—rage at the driver who'd killed her, rage at the paramedics who'd failed to save her, rage at the police for not doing enough, rage at Ivy for not reacting the way he thought she should, rage at God for allowing Emily to die, rage at Emily herself for getting plastered—on and on it went. Drinking had become his pain reliever, but if it was taking the edge off his grief, it was doing nothing for his anger. It simmered constantly beneath the surface and occasionally spilled over when he lashed out at some unsuspecting person in his path. Which was why Ivy was so nervous about this weekend. She didn't want Jim to jeopardize her future with *XCellNourish*. Maria might not want the liability of a manager who was married to an alcoholic. Ivy had made it clear to Jim before they left the house that he needed to keep himself in check and not overdo it, but that might prove challenging if everyone else was drinking. She'd considered having a quiet word with Maria about the situation, but she didn't want to be a party pooper. Bringing up Emily's tragic death was sure to put a damper on the weekend. After all, they were here to celebrate, not for grief counseling.

She fixed a smile in place as she greeted Brock and Ricki, and accepted a drink from Alex, pretending not to notice the death glare he gave Maria when she directed him to fill a bucket of ice. Despite the facade of congeniality, she sensed tension in the air from all quarters. Perhaps, she wasn't the only one worried about getting through the weekend. Margaritas in hand, they all wandered out to the deck and settled into Adirondack chairs.

"Doesn't get any better than this," Brock said, as he leaned back and gazed out at the lake. Ivy was surprised to see Ricki rebuff his attempt to reach for her hand. She must be peeved with him about something. Strike three for the perfect couple this weekend.

"We never get tired of the view," Maria said, setting down a serving platter of artichoke and jalapeño dip next to the pitcher of margaritas on the outdoor dining table. "Alex does his best writing up here, don't you honey?"

"If you say so, *dear*," he replied, keeping his back to her as he fired up the grill.

Ivy raised her brows and whispered to Jim. "A little too much volcanic activity in the kitchen, or what?"

Jim chuckled and chugged the last of his margarita. His eyes wandered longingly to the table where Maria had placed the pitcher.

Ivy opened her mouth to remind him to pace himself, but before she could say anything, Brock jumped up. "Here, let me top you off, buddy," he said. "I'll handle bar duties while Alex works his magic at the grill."

"Appreciate that, my man," Jim responded, holding his glass aloft.

After Brock had refilled his drink, Jim got to his feet. "I reckon it's time for a toast. Here's to the *XCellNourish* dream team, its talented founder, Maria Dalcerri, and her top-notch managerial crew, Ricki Wagner, and Ivy O'Shaughnessy!"

They all cheered and clinked their glasses before dissolving into the amiable chatter of the slightly inebriated. Ivy was thankful when Alex announced that the steaks were ready. She'd lost count of how many drinks Jim had consumed, but she was painfully aware that his laughter was growing more raucous by the minute. She joined the others at the dining table, her mouth watering at the delicious aroma of charred meat.

"Dig in everyone!" Maria said. As she reached for the salad bowl, her phone began to ring. "Do me a favor and pass that around," she said, handing the bowl to Ivy. She got up from the table and retreated to the far end of the patio to take the call. Ivy couldn't help noticing her brow crease as she talked with someone on the phone. Hopefully, it wasn't an urgent issue with the business. Maria was tethered to it night and day, as it was.

"Everything all right?" Ivy asked, when she rejoined them at the table, a few minutes later.

Maria twisted her lips as she speared a piece of succulent steak. "It was our crotchety neighbor, Larry Thompson. He lives in the A-frame cabin you passed on the way in. He says we're being too noisy, and he can't sleep. I invited him to join us, but he declined. It's always something with him. He just can't stand the fact that we have friends. He spies on every car that comes to our house, but I never see anyone visiting him. His wife left him years ago—supposedly he threatened her with a shotgun. The owner of the coffee shop in town says he doesn't speak to his kids either. They had some kind of falling out too."

"Want me to go knock on his door and sort him out for you?" Ivy suggested. "I could do a Ninja sales pitch on him that would make sure he never calls to complain again."

Maria laughed. "What do you think, Ricki? Should we subject him to an earful of Ivy?"

"Sure, if you want to reduce your neighbor to a shivering wreck," Ricki replied, with a strained smile.

Ivy smiled back, trying not to look unduly concerned. Ricki seemed a bit out of it this evening. She hadn't been herself at the monthly strategy meeting this morning either. She'd even left work early, which was unusual for her. Maybe she was coming down with something.

Ivy sipped her drink, one eye on Jim who was busy regaling Brock and Alex with some wild scuba diving debacle, snippets of which drifted her way. Jim was definitely the loudest one here, arms flailing in full blown reenactment mode. She hoped he didn't cause Maria any more grief with her neighbor. It sounded like he could be dangerous. A shiver crossed her shoulders, and she pulled her chair a little closer to the fire pit they had gathered around after dinner.

"Getting a little chilly, isn't it? Let me grab you a sweatshirt," Maria said. Without waiting for an answer, she set down her drink and disappeared into the house. Moments later, she reemerged with a gray hoodie in hand. "Here, throw this over your shoulders."

"Thanks," Ivy replied, grateful for the added warmth. Jim always teased her that she had the metabolism of an eighty-year-old—she was usually the first one to get cold.

"What are you guys cracking up about?" Maria asked Jim. "I feel like us girls are missing out on a good story."

Jim swatted a hand at her, his shoulders shaking with laughter. "Just some gnarly underwater power tool stuff. Trust me, you don't want to know."

Maria made a face. "Not fair—you're leaving us out. I have an idea. How about a round of *two truths and one lie*?"

Jim stared at her, looking like a chastened puppy, as he tossed back the contents of his glass.

Ivy grimaced at the suggestion. Anything too introspective tended to turn Jim's thoughts to Emily—which was why he stuck to being boisterous and horsing around. Brock didn't look too comfortable with the idea either. He was squirming in his seat like a schoolboy. Ivy was relieved when Alex spoke up and nixed the notion.

"This isn't a corporate retreat, Maria. I vote for another round of drinks instead."

Ivy glanced at her watch, hoping she could put the brakes on that idea. It was almost 11:30 p.m. "I hate to be the first one to call it a night but—"

"Then don't!" Jim cut in. "Tequila shots anyone?"

"I'm on it!" Alex replied, shooting to his feet.

Ivy sank back in her chair, resigning herself to the will of the group.

Moments later, she heard a car pull into the gravel driveway.

Ivy turned to Maria. "Kind of late for visitors, isn't it? Did you invite someone else?"

"Not unless Larry decided to get off his high horse and join us." The doorbell rang and Maria got to her feet, visibly frustrated. "He's probably here to complain."

She disappeared into the house, and Ivy edged her chair closer to the fire. Slipping her hands into the pockets of the hoodie she was wearing, her fingers curled around a small pill. She pulled it out and peered at it. *Zoloft.* Her mind whirred in confusion. Was the stress of the business getting to Maria?

Ivy dropped the antidepressant back into her pocket, shaken at the discovery. Maria was an outspoken advocate for all things natural in their national advertising campaign. If the press got a hold of this, it would be enough to send the stock of *XCellNourish* plummeting.

5

M aria climbed into bed fuming at her cantankerous old neighbor. She couldn't believe Larry had actually called the police on them—that was a first. They weren't even making that much noise. As she'd explained to the mostly sympathetic young officer who'd shown up at the door, they'd turned the music off at 10:00 p.m. and were simply sitting around the fire pit chatting. Larry really was a piece of work. If there was nothing to complain about, he'd make something up. He griped constantly about everyone and everything at the home association meetings. Lately, he'd even been spreading rumors about drug dealers casing the neighborhood. He actually threatened to pull his shotgun on any strangers who trespassed. It was him the police should be worried about.

Maria shivered and yanked the covers up to her chin. She hated that Larry had tried to spoil the celebratory weekend she'd planned for Ivy and Ricki and embarrassed her in front of her friends. Some people were bound and determined to be miserable and rain on everyone else's parade. There wasn't much she could do about it, other than buy him out—an idea she had entertained. She could raze the old cabin and build a vacation rental property in its place. It would be a good investment, and now that the company was booming, she could afford it. The hard part would be convincing Larry to sell. He had been here for over thirty years and acted like he owned this section of the lake. Despite the cool breeze drifting in from the open window, she tossed and turned for what felt like forever before finally falling into a troubled sleep.

It was light out when she woke with a start. She couldn't recall what the woman in her dream had been screaming about—probably nothing she cared to remember. Yawning, she turned over, anticipating sleeping in, for once. Her body tensed at what sounded like a frail voice calling for help. Her eyes shot open. Bolting out of bed, she ran to the window and peered out at the lake. She hadn't been dreaming. An elderly woman in a coat was stumbling up the beach toward the house with a dog in tow. She looked a little unsteady on her feet—maybe she'd taken a tumble or something.

Pulling a sweatshirt over her head, Maria darted downstairs and out the back door in her pajamas. She jogged down the deck steps and ran down the lawn toward the beach.

When she reached the elderly woman, she slid an arm around her shaking shoulders. "I heard you calling for help. Are you hurt?"

The woman shook her head in a jerky manner, her prunish lips wobbling as she tried to speak. "I ... I saw ... there's a body ... in the water."

Maria blinked, her brain still sluggish after being violently jerked into action. "You mean ... a *human* body?"

"Yes. Well, I think so," the woman wheezed, clearly winded from her attempt to hurry up the beach. "My dog was sniffing at something. It looked like a woman. I saw hair floating beneath the water." She fluttered her fingers to demonstrate.

"Where was this?" Maria asked, dubiously. She couldn't help wondering if the elderly woman had dementia. It was clear she'd had some kind of fright, but had she really seen a body? She sounded confused.

The woman pivoted and frowned in the direction of the water.

"I'm not sure where exactly. Over there, I think." She pointed to a dark patch of pondweed near the dock.

Maria hesitated. She was half tempted to run down to the water and check in the weeds herself. That way she might be able to reassure the woman that she'd mistaken a dead, bleached out fish for a human face. On the other hand, if there was any chance at all that there was a body in the weeds, it was the last thing Maria wanted to set eyes on before her morning cup of coffee.

"Okay, let's get you into the house and I'll have my husband take a look. I'm Maria, by the way. What's your name?"

"Angela Marshall. I live in the sub-division on the other side of the road." She let out a pitiful sob and lurched forward. "What a horrible thing to happen. That poor woman, she was someone's daughter."

Maria reached for Angela's elbow to support her, half-afraid she would collapse in the sand. "I want you to concentrate on yourself for now, Angela. We can't have you falling and breaking a bone. My husband, Alex, will take care of it."

Safely seated at the kitchen table, Angela curled her knotted fingers around the oversized mug of coffee Maria placed in front of her. She blinked up at her like a lost child. "I don't know what I should do. I can't think straight. Will you call the police for me, dear?"

Maria gulped down a few mouthfuls of coffee, relishing the instantaneous rush of brain lubrication. "Yes, of course. First things first. We need to confirm that you saw an actual body and not some inflatable toy or something. It's not that I don't believe you, but it wouldn't be the first time a burst flamingo got tangled up in our dock. It would be helpful to have someone verify what we're dealing with before we call the police. Why don't you sit tight and drink your coffee while I run upstairs and wake my husband?"

It took several minutes of vigorous shaking to rouse Alex from a deep slumber. He sat up and rubbed his eyes groggily. "What time is it? I thought we were sleeping in this morning."

"There's an elderly woman downstairs from the subdivision across the street. She was walking on the beach this morning and she says her Labrador found a body floating in the weeds by our dock. I need you to go check it out. I don't want to call the police if it turns out she's mistaken. She seems a bit confused, but she's adamant about seeing a body."

Alex groaned as he climbed out of bed. "It was probably just someone out for an early morning swim."

"In the pondweed? Unlikely." Maria tossed him a sweatshirt and jogging pants. "Go check it out."

She exited the bedroom to find Brock and Ricki huddled together at their bedroom door.

"Is everything all right?" Ricki asked, looking tentative. "Brock thought he heard a scream earlier."

"I'm not sure, to be honest." Maria lowered her voice. "There's an elderly woman in my kitchen. Her name's Angela. She says she saw a body floating in the pondweed when she was walking her dog. Alex is going to check it out. It's probably nothing. She's got to be in her eighties—I'm not sure how good her eyesight is."

Ricki clutched nervously at her throat before turning to Brock. "You should go with Alex, just in case."

"In case what?"

"I don't know." Ricki glared at him. "In case Alex needs help."

Brock scratched the stubble on his jaw before casting a resigned look in Maria's direction. "Okay, sure. I'll walk down there with him."

The door to Ivy's and Jim's room opened, and Ivy stuck her head out. She looked around sleepily, her forehead rumpling. "What's going on? Why's everyone up already?"

Maria repeated what she'd told Brock and Ricki. "I need to go back downstairs and check on Angela. She's pretty shook up. I should probably offer her something to eat."

"I'll wake Jim," Ivy said. "I'll be right down to help you."

"No need to wake him, yet," Maria assured her. "It might turn out to be nothing." She hurried back down the stairs before Ivy could argue the point. The last thing she needed was a hungover Jim in the mix stirring things up. It hadn't escaped her notice that he'd drunk twice as much as anyone else last night and been five times as loud.

When Maria entered the kitchen, Angela was staring blankly at the refrigerator, still clutching her untouched mug of coffee. Her eyes twitched in Maria's direction. "Oh, you're back, dear. What ... what did the police say?"

Maria fixed a patient smile on her face. "My husband's going down to the water right now. Once he locates the body, we'll call the police. You should drink your coffee, Angela. It will do you good to get something warm in your stomach. You've had a terrible shock. Would you like something to eat?"

"I'm not that hungry." Angela looked down at Duke who was stretched out at her feet, resting his grey, bristled jaw on his paws. "I don't suppose you have any dog food, do you? I'm not sure how long it will take the police to get here, and Duke's used to getting his breakfast at the same time every morning."

"I don't have any dog food, but I was going to cook some bacon for breakfast. Can he have some of that?"

Angela's face brightened. "Oh yes! He'd love that! Thank you, dear." Her brow furrowed. "Do you know that woman who drowned? Someone should let her family know what happened."

Maria opened her mouth to remind her that she hadn't seen the woman but thought better of it. Angela was just forgetful enough to cast doubt on her story, but not enough for Maria to dismiss it entirely. "I'm sure the police will take care of notifying her family once they get here," she soothed.

Alex walked into the kitchen and nodded a terse greeting to Angela before leaning over to whisper to Maria. "Where exactly did she say she saw this body?"

Maria guided him by the elbow out to the back deck and pointed to a dark patch of pondweed. "Right over there. She seemed a little unsure so take a look all around the dock area just to be safe."

Brock came walking out and joined them, arching his back and stretching his arms above his head. "Rough way to start the morning. I'm sure it will turn out to be nothing. Lead the way, Alex."

Maria headed back inside the house just as Ivy came down the stairs. "Jim's up," she said. "All the commotion woke him. He'll be right down. What can I do to help?"

"You can sit with Angela while I make her dog something to eat, if you want," Maria replied.

Back in the kitchen, she pulled out a pan to fry some bacon. She didn't feel like eating, and she doubted anyone else would either if they actually discovered a body in the weeds, but she needed to do something. She'd never been the type to sit around twiddling her thumbs. If feeding Duke was Angela's primary concern, then at least she could ease the poor woman's mind on that front.

Moments later, Jim stepped into the kitchen looking considerably worse for wear. His hair was sticking up in wiry clumps and his eyes were bloodshot. Maria pressed her lips together in disapproval as he slumped into the seat opposite Ivy and rubbed his hands over his face. She was no prude when it came to enjoying a few drinks, but she was a firm believer in knowing your limit and sticking to it. She couldn't help wondering if Emily's death had contributed to his tendency to overindulge—he'd been so angry at the funeral and said some crazy things. Ivy hadn't confided in her much in the aftermath of the accident. She'd taken a few weeks off work and then got right back into the swing of things.

"Where are Alex and Brock?" Jim asked.

"Down at the water," Ivy replied.

Jim made as if to get up from the table, but Ivy laid a hand on his arm. "Don't go," she said firmly. "They'll fetch you if they need you."

Maria knew she was only trying to protect her husband. Seeing his daughter's body in the morgue had broken him. The last thing he needed was to come face-to-face with another young woman who had died before her time.

Maria finished frying the bacon and let it cool for a couple of minutes before feeding a few slices to Duke. The dog scarfed it down and then looked up at her with a hopeful expression in his treacle-colored eyes. "Sorry buddy," she said, placing the pan in the sink. "I need to save some for my company, just in case anyone's hungry."

"Thank you dear," Angela said, rubbing Duke's head affectionately. "That was very thoughtful of you."

Maria had just set down a bowl of water next to the dog when she heard footsteps coming up the steps to the back deck. Her stomach knotted. She left the frying pan soaking in the sink and hurried out to meet Alex and Brock. "Did you find anything?" she blurted out, wrapping her arms tightly around her body. It wasn't even cold out, but a creeping sensation in her gut was making her shiver. The dark expression on her husband's face told her everything she needed to know.

"We should talk inside," he muttered.

Maria followed him and an ashen Brock into the kitchen and sank down at the table next to the others. For a long moment they said nothing, exchanging anguished looks with one another.

"Did you find anything?" Angela asked, at last.

"It's not good," Brock said, his lip wobbling. He stared morosely across the table at no one in particular.

"Just spit it out, man!" Jim blustered. "If I've been dragged out of bed at an unearthly hour, it better be for a good reason." He folded his arms across his burly chest and leaned back in his chair expectantly.

"Alex, tell us, please!" Maria pressed.

He rubbed a hand over his jaw and looked nervously around the taut faces. "We found a woman's body."

6

Detective Dan Palmer swept an admiring gaze over the opulent stone-clad lake house that he and Officer Mateo Lopez had just pulled up outside. An expansive wall of windows on both the front and back of the house captured the view through to the lakeside. A picture-perfect setting—except for the body that had, apparently, washed up overnight. It seemed like every summer there were at least one or two drownings, and with the lake growing busier every year, the number of fatalities was on the rise. Most were accidental, with the occasional suicide. This season had started out early with the tragic drowning of a toddler the first week of May. Palmer steeled himself as he approached the front door. It was already gearing up to be a deadly year on the water.

"Prime location they've got here," Lopez commented, as he rang the doorbell.

Palmer nodded. "The woman who discovered the body doesn't live here. The owner heard her screaming on the beach and brought her back to the house once she heard what had happened."

Lopez grunted. "Not the best way to wake up on a Saturday morning."

The paneled door swung open, and Palmer found himself

looking at a trim woman with vanilla-colored hair and flawless skin. It was hard to pinpoint her exact age—fortyish, if he had to hazard a guess—but it was evident she worked out and took good care of herself. Even without any make up, she was attractive, despite the worry lines on her face.

Palmer flashed his ID. "I'm Detective Dan Palmer with the Nevada Sheriff's department." He gestured to his right. "This is my partner, Officer Lopez."

"I'm Maria Dalcerri, the homeowner," the woman replied, stepping aside. "Please come in." She led them through to the expansive kitchen and introduced them to the small somber-faced group assembled inside. A scent of bacon hung in the air. An odd thing to cook when you've just discovered a body, Palmer thought, as he did a discreet assessment of his surroundings. Judging by the margarita glasses lined up next to the sink, and the haggard-looking faces angled in his direction, the group had been partying hard last night. He'd suspected as much. The officer on duty at the station had been called out on a noise complaint lodged by a neighbor.

Palmer's gaze came to rest on an elderly woman seated at the table, with a heavyset black lab at her feet. Several decades older than the rest of the party, she stuck out like a sore thumb—not to mention the fact that she was the only one dressed for the outdoors. He was guessing she was the unfortunate soul who'd found the body.

"The medical examiner's on his way," he informed them. "Does someone want to take us to the body?"

"My husband will, he knows where it is," Maria answered, nodding a command to Alex. A look of revulsion flitted across his face.

Palmer couldn't be sure if it was triggered by the thought of seeing the body again or being ordered about by his wife. After a moment's hesitation, Alex got to his feet and gestured for the officers to follow him.

Palmer hesitated on the back deck for a moment to take in the breathtaking view. The surface of the water glittered in the morning sun as though strewn with diamonds, the wind pushing it ever so gently westward. A boat traveling in the opposite direction left a cotton white trail in its wake—deceptively idyllic. Palmer was only too aware that the lake was a grim reaper that should never be underestimated.

"Quite the view you've got here," Officer Lopez said, as they made their way over the sand.

"Won't be the same after this," Alex muttered darkly. He led them to the water's edge and pointed at a shaded patch of pondweed near the dock, before folding his arms across his chest. "The body's over there. If it's all the same to you, I'd rather wait here."

Palmer stepped ankle deep into the lake and waded out to the patch of weeds in question. As he peered down into the water, a milky white face with lifeless eyes stared back up at him—a young woman. Early twenties, if he had to guess. He was no medical expert, but it was clear she hadn't been in the water for long. Her pale fingers were entangled in the weeds, her perfect white tips intact. Palmer recognized the French manicure his daughter had worn for her wedding in the spring. His gut tightened at the realization that she was about the dead woman's age.

"Fully clothed. She wasn't out for a late-night swim, boss," Lopez said in a low voice. "What do you reckon?"

Palmer grimaced. "Could have been an accident. You know how well drinking and boating go together."

"Except no one's been reported missing. Makes me think someone doesn't want her to be found."

Palmer hefted a brow and nodded approvingly. "This is exactly why you're going to make a wonderful detective, Lopez."

He glanced up as people began streaming across the sand. The medical examiner's team had arrived to retrieve the body. They'd be able to make an initial assessment and check for any obvious injuries. He greeted the medical examiner, Jack Malone, as CSI techs began assembling a privacy tent on the beach.

"The looky-loos are already kayaking by at a snail's pace trying to get an eyeful," Jack grumbled.

"That's as close as they'll get," Palmer replied. "I'll have Lopez cordon off this section of the beach. I'm going to head back up to the house and start interviewing the witnesses. Let me know right away if you find anything suspicious, or any ID on the body. I'd like to be able to notify next-of-kin before the media gets a hold of this."

He turned to Lopez and began rattling off instructions. "Make sure no one accesses the beach while the ME and his team are working. You'll have to call for backup—we'll need a couple more officers out here. Take a look around the exterior of the house for anything suspicious, any signs of a scuffle, that kind of thing. We need to rule out any connection between the dead girl and the party that took place here last night. And see if you can get someone at the station to email you a copy of that noise complaint. I want to know if there was any report of an argument or raised voices."

Back in the house, Palmer made a beeline for Maria. "Do you have a quiet spot somewhere where I can talk in private to the woman who discovered the body?"

"Sure," Maria said, showing him into the sunroom overlooking the beach. "This is where Alex does most of his writing. He enjoys the lake breeze on this side of the house. I'll fetch Angela for you."

She returned, a moment later, with the elderly woman leaning on her arm, her Lab trotting faithfully behind them.

"I'll be in the kitchen if you need anything," Maria said, closing the door behind her.

"How are you holding up, Angela?" Palmer asked, regarding the elderly woman perched on the couch opposite him. "I realize this has been a traumatic morning for you. I can have a paramedic check you out, if you'd like."

"Oh no, that won't be necessary, thanks. I'm doing much better now," Angela replied, absentmindedly stroking her dog's head. "But I have to admit, it was a terrible shock."

"I'm sure it was. Can you describe for me how you discovered the body?"

Angela's brow creased. "Well, I walk Duke at the same time every morning. He likes the routine, you see. I suppose we both do." She let out a melancholy chuckle. "That's what happens when you're old and set in your ways."

Palmer smiled patiently as he waited for her to continue.

"Once we reach the sand, I usually let Duke off the leash for a few minutes, if there's no one else around. Although, it's getting to be more difficult for me with my arthritis these days. The clasp is stiff." Instinctively, she rubbed a thumb over her knotted knuckles. "The doctor says—"

"I take it Duke found the body?" Palmer interrupted.

Angela nodded thoughtfully. "That poor girl's mother. I can't imagine finding out that your baby girl has drowned. It's heartbreaking. I have two sons, and they're both strong swimmers. I made them take lessons when—"

"Heartbreaking indeed," Palmer cut in. "Did you recognize the woman?"

Angela shook her head. "No. I've never seen her before. She doesn't live around here. I know all the locals."

"Do you live nearby?" Palmer asked, jotting down a couple of notes.

"Yes. In the subdivision across the way. We have an easement down to the water and a shared dock. It's a public beach so everyone walks their dogs on it."

"Got it. How well do you know Maria and Alex Dalcerri?"

Angela pursed her lips. "Not well at all. They're part timers. He spends more time up here than she does. Jacintha, who works in the coffee shop in town, tells me he's a writer. I believe Maria owns some big-shot health company. That's the way it is these days, isn't it, the women make the money." Duke whined and got to his feet, nuzzling her. Angela looked imploringly at Palmer. "If that's all you need from me, I'd like to go home now. Duke's been very patient, but he's getting hungry."

"Not a problem at all. We have your number if we have any additional questions. Would you like Officer Lopez to drive you home?"

"That's very kind of you, but it's only over the road. I'm the first house in the sub-division."

After escorting Angela and Duke to the door, Palmer returned to the kitchen where Maria and Alex were seated at opposite ends of the table in a cold fog of silence. Palmer pulled out his notebook and joined them. "Where are your guests?"

"They went back upstairs to get dressed," Maria answered.

Palmer nodded. "I have an initial statement from Angela Marshall. How about you give me a rundown of what happened from your perspective?"

Alex looked pointedly at Maria. She cleared her throat and began. "I woke up when I heard a scream. At first, I thought I was dreaming, but then I heard someone calling for help. We sleep with the windows open to let the cool air in. I jumped out of bed and ran to the window. That's when I saw an elderly woman stumbling across the sand toward the house. I thought she might have fallen and hurt herself, or something, so I hurried outside to help her." Maria frowned, as though recalling the moment.

"Go on," Palmer prompted.

"She told me she'd seen a body in the water near the dock. To be honest, I didn't know whether to believe her, at first. I thought maybe she was mistaken—that she'd seen a dead fish caught in the weeds."

"Did you look for the body?"

Maria shook her head. "Angela was in bad shape, so I helped her up to the house. Then, I woke my husband and sent him down to take a look. Isn't that right, Alex?"

Palmer turned his attention to Maria's husband—a trim, sandy haired, attractive-looking man. Except for his expression. He appeared to be traumatized by what he'd encountered. It wasn't uncommon to freak out when you saw a dead person. Palmer would never forget the first time he'd set eyes on a corpse in a murder investigation. He hadn't slept for a week afterward. He fixed a sympathetic smile on his face as he addressed Alex. "Rough, isn't it?"

Alex gave a perfunctory nod and dropped his gaze. "I spend a lot of time up here at the lake. Nothing like this has ever happened before."

"What do you do for a living?"

"I'm an author. I write thrillers."

Palmer raised his brows a fraction. He was pretty sure writing wouldn't fund a second home of this caliber—not unless you were a household name. "What do you do for work?" he asked, turning to Maria.

She threw him an irritated look as though she found the question demeaning. "I own a nutritional supplement company called *XCell-Nourish*."

Palmer jotted down the name. He'd never heard of it. He would look it up later and see what he could find out about it. "And the other couples, are they friends of yours?"

"Ricki and Ivy both work for me," Maria replied. "I invited them and their spouses to spend the weekend at the lake with us. It was a reward of sorts to celebrate our most successful quarter to date."

"Congratulations," Palmer said, as he checked his notes. "I understand one of your neighbors filed a noise complaint last night."

Maria tightened her lips in displeasure. "That was Larry next door. We weren't disturbing anybody. He's always griping about something or other." She gestured toward the empty glasses stacked by the sink. "Alex made margaritas and grilled some steaks. We sat out on the back deck and talked and enjoyed the sunset. That was the height of the noise disturbance."

"Did you see or hear anything unusual?"

"No. Nothing at all."

Palmer turned his attention back to Alex. "Did you recognize the deceased woman when you located the body?"

Alex shook his head, but Palmer didn't miss the tight set of his jaw as he did so. His shifty mannerism smacked of deception. "What about your friend who accompanied you down to the water? Did he have any idea who the woman was?"

"He's more of an acquaintance," Alex responded. "His wife works for Maria. But no, he didn't know her either."

Palmer pinned his gaze on Maria. "Would you be willing to take a look at a photo of the woman, once the medical examiner is through with his initial examination? If she doesn't have any ID on her, we're going to be relying on someone recognizing her in order to identify her."

Maria squeezed the water bottle she was holding, flinching when it crackled. "I don't relish the thought, but I'll do what I can to help."

Palmer set down his pen and leaned back in his chair. "I appreciate your cooperation. That's all I need from you for now. Let me talk to Brock and his wife next." He glanced down at his notebook. "Ivy? Or is it Ricki?"

"Ricki," Maria confirmed. "I'll fetch them."

BROCK AND RICKI WAGNER took a seat at the kitchen table looking pale and exhausted.

"Thanks for giving me a few minutes of your time," Palmer began. "I realize this is a very distressing situation for everyone involved."

"It's awful," Ricki agreed, her voice trailing off. "I can't believe it. It's like a bad dream." She swept an anxious look over Brock. "My husband's still reeling from the shock of finding the body."

Palmer turned his attention to Brock. "Did you recognize the woman?"

"I would have said something by now, if I had, wouldn't I?" Brock shot back, tightening his jaw.

Palmer blinked thoughtfully. His reaction seemed a little extreme for such a routine question. Still, shock could do strange things to a person.

"She looks young, I'm guessing early twenties," Palmer went on. "The sooner we identify her, the sooner we can notify her parents."

Ricki's eyes clouded over. "I can't imagine having to bury a child." She chewed nervously on her lip. "I should warn you that Ivy and Jim lost their only child a couple of months ago. She'd just turned twenty-three. This is going to trigger some awful memories for them."

Palmer softened his expression. "I appreciate you letting me know. I'll do my best to handle them with kid gloves."

"That's all I need from you for now," he said, slapping his thighs and getting to his feet. I'll be in touch if I think of anything else."

"Does that mean we're free to go?" Brock asked, a feverish look in his eyes.

Palmer furrowed his brow. "I can appreciate that you're eager to get out of here, but I'd like everyone to hang around until I've had a chance to speak to the medical examiner. I might need you to take a look at a photo of the woman, if we can't find any ID on her."

Brock wet his lips, sliding Palmer a nervous look as he followed his wife out of the room.

When the door closed behind them, Palmer let out a long breath. The couples he'd interviewed so far were decidedly ill-at-ease. Something didn't feel right, but he couldn't put his finger on what it was. Until he could rule out foul play, he wasn't going to let the group disperse. There was a possibility the dead girl had been partying with them last night, and that something had gone amok. Alex and Brock hadn't been at all convincing when they'd denied knowing who she was.

After all, this was the second time the police had been called out to the house in the past twenty-four hours, and Palmer wasn't a big believer in coincidences.

7

S eated opposite the third couple, Ivy and Jim O'Shaughnessy, Palmer pegged Jim as a heavy drinker. It wasn't hard to deduce from his puffy face and bloodshot eyes that he'd indulged pretty heavily the previous evening.

"Thanks for assisting with the investigation," Palmer began. "This will only take a few minutes of your time."

Jim folded his arms in front of him and leaned back, his dark eyes slashes of defiance. "You call this an investigation? You cops are a joke. I could do a better job myself."

Palmer kept his expression neutral. He'd dealt with enough belligerent drunks to know when they were trying to pick a fight—far better to let him sputter until he'd run out of steam.

"Please don't start, Jim," Ivy pleaded. "Let the detective ask his questions and then we can get out of here."

Palmer gave an appreciative nod. "I just need to confirm a couple of things. Jim, I understand you were asleep when Maria brought Angela back to the house. How did you find out about what had happened?"

Jim's lips remained fastened shut. An uncomfortable silence descended, broken only by Officer Lopez's soft footfall as he slipped into the room. Palmer gave him a brief nod of acknowledgement, quickly returning a questioning gaze to Jim.

"I heard a commotion, someone going up and down the stairs," Ivy volunteered. "I came out to see what was going on and that's when Maria told me about the woman out walking her dog who'd stumbled across a body in the water. I woke Jim, and we went downstairs. Poor Angela was sitting at the kitchen table looking half scared to death. We were a bit skeptical that she'd really seen a body, so Brock and Alex went down to the water to take a look."

"And you remained at the house?" Palmer asked, turning back to Jim.

Ivy cleared her throat and spoke up once again. "I ... didn't want Jim to go with them. We lost our daughter recently, and I was afraid it would bring back bad memories. It's been difficult, as you can imagine."

"I'm sorry for your loss," Palmer said.

"Sorry?" Jim echoed in a tone laced with loathing. "That's all you got? You cops screwed up big time when my daughter's killer slipped through the cracks of your lousy *investigation*."

"Stop it, Jim!" Ivy chided, laying a hand on his arm. "This has nothing to do with Emily."

Jim shrugged her off, half-rising out of his seat. "It has everything to do with her! It's the same old story. They never catch the killer. What good are you anyway?" he bellowed. "A sorry waste of taxpayer dollars!"

Ivy shook her head apologetically at Palmer. "Our daughter stepped out in front of a car. She'd been drinking, and the autopsy determined there were drugs in her system."

"Our Emily didn't do drugs—you know that! And the bartender said she only had two drinks." Jim jabbed an accusing finger in Palmer's direction. "The cops never even tried to find out how she ingested the drugs. Her drink was spiked! You're useless—clowns, the lot of you." He lumbered toward Palmer, flexing a fist, his face clouding over like a thunderstorm.

"Jim, that's enough!" Ivy cried. "Cut it out!"

"Sir, I'm going to have to cuff you if you don't back away," Officer Lopez said, stepping toward Jim and reaching a hand behind him for his handcuffs.

"That won't be necessary, officer," Ivy said, tugging her husband by the arm in an attempt to get him to sit back down. Scowling, he brushed her off and stomped out of the room.

"Want me to follow him, boss?" Lopez asked.

Palmer shook his head. "He didn't see the body, there's nothing more he can tell us."

"I'm so sorry," Ivy said, wringing her hands. "This is really hard for him. He never got over Emily's death. He lashes out at everyone. He's convinced someone spiked her drink that night. I suppose it's possible. Maybe some guy was hitting on her and slipped something into Emily's drink." Ivy gave a resigned shake of her head. "It's pointless living in the past when there's nothing you can do to change things. I treasure my memories of our daughter and the good times we had. But for Jim, it's a festering wound he insists on picking at. He can't accept that he'll never get to walk her down the aisle or play with his grandchildren."

Palmer tightened his jaw. "I feel for him. I have two daughters myself—both married with kids now. If anything ever happened to them, it would tear me apart."

He glanced up at a sharp knock on the back door. Officer Lopez opened it and exchanged a few words with one of the medical techs.

"Jack wants to speak with you, boss," Lopez said, raising a meaningful brow.

Palmer stood abruptly. "Thanks for your time, Ivy. This shouldn't take too much longer and then you'll be free to go."

She got to her feet and gave a shaky smile. "Thanks for being so understanding about Jim's behavior."

"Not a problem," Palmer replied, exiting the kitchen.

"WHAT DID THE TECH SAY?" he muttered to Lopez as they jogged down the deck steps to the beach.

"Not much. Just that Jack needs to show you something before they pack up."

"You know what that means, don't you?" Palmer prompted.

"It means those couples aren't going home any time soon," Lopez answered cryptically.

Palmer grunted. "Their chances just decreased—I'll give you that."

As they approached the pop-up crime scene tent on the beach, Palmer steeled himself for bad news. He'd been hoping this would turn out to be a straightforward drowning—in the sense that no foul play was involved—but Jack had obviously found something that merited his attention. He ducked into the tent where he found the ME bent over the corpse of the young woman, peering into her ears.

"What have you got for me?" Palmer asked in a grim tone.

"Ah, there you are!" Jack straightened up and placed one hand on the small of his back. "I'm getting too old for this line of work. It's time I applied for an office job."

"You'd hate every minute of it, and you know it," Palmer replied. "What did you want to show me?"

"It's nothing conclusive, yet. By the looks of things, she's only been in the water four or five hours at most. I need to get her back to the lab to do a tox exam. But check out this contusion on the right side of her head."

Palmer and Lopez bent down and studied the discolored area Jack was pointing to.

"Could this have been caused by a fall, hitting her head on the side of the dock, or a boat?" Lopez asked.

"It's possible," Jack agreed. He raised his shaggy brows as he peeled off his gloves. "Or someone could have clocked her on the side of the head."

"And in your expert opinion, which of those options is it?" Palmer asked.

"It wouldn't be my expert opinion if I were to speculate, would it?" Jack pushed his glasses up his ruddy nose and grinned at him. "I'll give you my verdict once I get her back to the lab. But I thought you'd want to know the possibility of foul play is now in play—pun intended."

Palmer grimaced. "There was some kind of raucous party on the back deck here last night. I can't help wondering if this woman was a casualty of it."

8

After taking a couple of closeup pictures of the deceased woman's face, Palmer and Lopez trudged back up the beach to the Dalcerris' house. Buried among the trees to the right, Palmer spotted a decrepit-looking A-frame cabin. Not much more than a roofline and a teetering chimney were visible from the beach, which wouldn't allow much of a view of the lake from the house. Palmer guessed this was the neighbor who had lodged the noise complaint. He'd pay him a visit next and see if he recognized the dead woman. To the left of the Dalcerris' place was an empty lot and beyond that the easement to the shared dock for the subdivision across the street.

"Pretty quiet down at this end of the lake," Palmer remarked. "Our only real chance of finding out what happened to that young woman is if the Dalcerris, or one of their friends, saw or heard something."

"We can rule out a late-night swim—fully dressed, with a contusion on her head—that sets off alarm bells, right off the bat," Lopez said.

Palmer grimaced. "I'm going to interview each of the couples again—show them a photo of the woman and see how they react."

"What about the neighbor?" Lopez asked, gesturing with his chin to the A-frame cabin. "The grouchy one who said he couldn't sleep with all the racket going on."

"We'll hit him up too. Did you get hold of the noise complaint report?"

"Yeah, nothing noteworthy. The neighbor claimed they were partying, and drinking, and generally being rowdy. The officer who followed up on it said the house was quiet when he arrived on the scene. No black eyes, and nothing untoward. The woman who greeted him at the door—Maria Dalcerri—was very polite and explained that her neighbor tended to be difficult."

Palmer grunted as they climbed the steps to the back deck. "Define difficult. If there's a booming bass next door keeping me awake half the night, I could become difficult too."

Lopez chuckled as he pushed open the back door and stepped inside. "I'd hate to be your neighbor, boss. I like my music loud."

After requesting to talk to each of the couples again, in turn, Palmer and Lopez retreated to the sunroom with Maria and Alex.

"What's this about?" Alex demanded.

"I'd like you both to take a look at a photo of the deceased woman and see if you recognize her," Palmer replied.

"I already told you, I don't know her," Alex protested, his face rigid. "I'd rather not look at her again. It's disturbing."

"As I explained earlier, I appreciate your assistance," Palmer went on. "I understand this is a difficult situation, especially with a house full of guests. Maria, perhaps you could take a look at the photograph, first."

She gave a tight nod, a flicker of apprehension traversing her features.

Palmer fished out his phone and pulled up a close-up of the woman's face. He passed the phone to Maria and watched her expression carefully as she examined it. After a moment or two, she shook her head in defeat and held out the phone to him. "I'm sorry, I've never seen her before. I have no idea who she is."

"Alex, I'd like you to take a look at the photo, too," Palmer said. "I imagine it was hard for you to see her features clearly in the water."

Alex passed a shaking hand over his forehead and reached for the phone. He glanced briefly at the screen and then swallowed hard. "No. I don't recognize her." He handed the phone back without meeting Palmer's gaze. Palmer shot Lopez a loaded look. Alex had barely glanced at the photo. Was he really that queasy about looking at a dead woman? Or was guilt driving him to rid himself of the sight of her as quickly as possible?

"Was the medical examiner able to give you any more information about how she died?" Maria asked, a pained expression on her face.

Palmer pressed his lips together. "I'm afraid I'm not at liberty to share any preliminary findings with you. We'll release a statement as soon as possible."

Maria's brows elevated ever so slightly, as though she'd deduced from what he'd said that the medical examiner had found something questionable. She was obviously intuitive, but nothing about her demeanor struck him as suspicious. Then again, she was a cool customer—nothing like her husband who looked like he was about to pass out.

"What time did the party end last night?" Palmer asked, flicking through his notes.

Maria let out a snort. "Thanks to ratchet-head next door, the police stopped by around ten-thirty, but we didn't have any music playing at that point. I think we went to bed around 1:00 a.m."

"Are you sure you didn't see or hear any activity around your dock?"

Maria shook her head. "Nothing. We slept hard last night. I didn't hear a thing until Angela's scream this morning." She turned to her husband. "I don't think you moved all night long. I had to shake you awake."

Alex grunted in agreement. "I was in a dead sleep." He gulped, his cheeks reddening as he realized what he'd said. "Sorry, poor choice of words."

Palmer flashed him a commiserative smile and then gave Officer Lopez a small nod to let him know he was about to wrap up the interview. "How long are you two up here for?"

"We were planning on staying until Sunday afternoon," Maria replied. "Actually, Alex was going to stay on for the week to do some writing." She blinked questioningly at her husband. "Although, after what's happened, we might be revisiting our plans. I'm not sure the other couples are going to want to spend another night here, under the circumstances."

Palmer rubbed his chin. "We'll need them to stay here for the next hour or so until the medical examiner and his team finish up, in case we have any additional questions. I'd appreciate it if you two could continue to play host as best you can, until then."

"Of course," Maria replied, firing a sharp look at Alex.

Palmer watched them exit the room, noting their body language. It was apparent that Maria led the charge—at the office and at home. Alex seemed to be perpetually at her beck and call. At least, that was the impression Palmer got. But impressions could be manipulated, and Alex Dalcerri was a storyteller, after all. Maybe in life as well as in print.

Palmer smiled politely as Brock and Ricki entered the room next and settled into the couch opposite him. The dynamic in their relationship was a little harder to decipher. He'd noticed that they had a habit of deferring to one another when Palmer directed questions at them. Ricki appeared more nervous than the other women, but Brock appeared to be even more shook up about the situation than she was. Maybe they were the sensitive ones in the group.

"I'd like you to take a look at this photo of the deceased woman and tell me if you recognize her," Palmer said, offering them his phone.

Ricki squeezed her husband's arm, encouraging him to reach for it. Palmer observed the tremor in his fingers as he took hold of the device. He blinked once at the screen and then quickly looked away.

Ricki leaned over and frowned at the screen before throwing Palmer a helpless look. "No, I'm sorry. I don't recognize her."

Brock handed Palmer back the phone. "I've no idea who she is either. I've never seen her before," he said shakily. "I don't know anyone in this neighborhood. This is the first time I've ever been up to the Dalcerris' lake house."

Palmer nodded, evaluating Brock's answer in his head. Overkill always smacked of desperation. Why hadn't he simply said he didn't recognize the woman?

"Did you hear or see anyone else on the beach last night?" Palmer asked, looking pointedly at Brock.

He shook his head. "No. Alex says it's always quiet at this end of the lake. The schools aren't out for another week, it picks up some after that."

"We didn't see anyone on the shared dock either," Ricki added. A distraught expression settled on her face. "It's so horrible to think about it. That poor woman. I hope you find out what happened to her."

"We'll do our best to get to the bottom of it," Palmer assured her, snapping his notebook shut. "That's all I need from you for now. I'll talk to the O'Shaughnessys briefly, and then Lopez and I will go next door and speak with the Dalcerris' neighbor. We should be able to get you out of here sometime in the next couple of hours." He nodded his thanks to Ricki and Brock as they exited the room.

JIM O'SHAUGHNESSY SCOWLED AT HIM, as he and Ivy took their seats. "How much longer are we going to be stuck here?" he blurted out before Palmer had a chance to speak.

"Not long, we're in the process of trying to identify the woman," Palmer explained, passing them his phone. "Do you recognize her at all?"

Ivy held the device close to her nose and peered at it. "I'm not trying to be morbid, I don't have my contacts in." After a moment or two, she shook her head and passed the phone to her husband. "Sorry, she doesn't look familiar."

Jim grasped the phone in his massive fist and curled the corners of his lips. "No idea. I've never seen her before."

Palmer made a few notes. Either Jim and Ivy were excellent liars, or they really had no idea who this woman was or what had happened to her.

Jim narrowed his eyes as he handed Palmer back his phone. "You're not gonna find out who killed her. You never do."

Ivy elbowed him in the ribs and gave him an icy glare.

Ignoring the jab, Palmer continued. "Did either of you hear or see anything out of the ordinary last night?"

"Nothing," Ivy confirmed, "Other than a car pulling up on the gravel a little before 11:00 p.m. That's when the police knocked on the door. Maria's neighbor called to complain that we were making too much noise. Which was completely bogus, of course. He's a dangerous character, by the sound of it." Ivy hesitated, a frown forming on her face. "Come to think of it, calling the police on your neighbor is the perfect way to pin a crime on them, isn't it?'

9

"This place looks a bit run down for this neighborhood," Lopez commented, as he and Palmer drove up a rutted driveway to the ramshackle cabin neighboring the Dalcerris' luxurious lake house.

"Can't imagine the Dalcerris are too happy about it," Palmer replied, as he climbed out of the squad car and surveyed his surroundings. "He doesn't even bother mowing his lawn, by the looks of it. No wonder they don't get along."

The wooden siding on the cabin was rotting in parts and in dire need of a coat of sealant. The overgrown yard was a minefield of abandoned parts, bags of trash, and rusty machinery infiltrated with weeds. An old Dodge truck was parked on what had presumably been a lawn at one time. On the front porch sat a badly frayed deck chair covered in bat excrement. Cobwebs coated every surface on the overhang.

"Not a welcoming sight, is it?" Palmer muttered under his breath as he gingerly stepped onto the rickety deck.

"Perfect setting for a slasher movie, if you ask me," Lopez added with a shudder.

After searching in vain for a doorbell, Palmer opened the torn screen and rapped his knuckles on the splintered door. Several minutes went by with no indication that anyone was coming. Ivy's words lingered in his ear: *calling the police on your neighbor is the perfect way to pin a crime on them.* He couldn't help wondering if she might be on to something. It wouldn't be all that surprising if the occupant of this house turned out to be a killer. He walked over to the nearest window and tented his fingers over his eyes to peer through the filthy glass. "I don't see any signs of life. But his truck's here, he's got to be close by. Why don't you walk around the side of the house and see if he's out on the back deck?"

Lopez strode off and reappeared a few minutes later. "Negative. Nothing but a scrawny-looking cat with one eye that hissed at me like a snake."

Palmer knocked on the glass and then went back to the front door and hammered on it with his fist. "Mr. Thompson? Anyone home?" he yelled. He was rewarded, a moment later, by the sound of footsteps shuffling toward the door. It creaked inward, and a narrow-faced man in his seventies peered out at them. His calculating gaze ran up and down the length of them.

"I'm Detective Dan Palmer and this is my partner, Officer Mateo Lopez," Palmer said, tipping his hat to him. "Are you Mr. Thompson?"

The door remained firmly in place, cracked open a mere inch or two. The man's nose twitched suspiciously, like a rabbit assessing a threat. "You following up on the noise complaint?"

"Yes and no," Palmer replied. "You are Larry Thompson, right?"

The man gave a cautious nod.

"Can we come in for a few minutes, Larry? You don't mind if I call you Larry, do you?"

His jaw slid silently back-and-forth as he weighed the requests. A moment later, Palmer heard the door scraping over the tile floor as it opened as far as the warped wood would permit. He turned his six-foot-three frame sideways and squeezed through the opening, followed by Lopez. Larry led them through to a dingy kitchen and motioned to them to take a seat at the table. Palmer sucked in his breath as he sat down on a beat-up wooden chair, wondering if it would hold his weight. He glanced around the gloomy interior, mentally cataloguing his surroundings. Every inch of counter space was taken up with a menagerie of boxes, appliances, dried pantry goods, paperwork, and every other miscellaneous item you could think of.

Palmer couldn't imagine what the inside of the cabinets looked like if so much stuff had overflowed onto the counters. Dust was layered throughout, and the tile floor looked like it hadn't been mopped in decades. For that matter, Larry looked like he hadn't bathed for decades either. His greasy hair—what was left of it—clung to a shiny scalp mottled with liver spots. He was wearing a pair of plastic slide-in sandals, his warped, yellow toenails on full display. Palmer wrinkled his nose with distaste. After twenty years on the force, he was no lightweight when it came to nauseating sights, but there was something about toenail fungus that hit a nerve with him.

Larry flicked a hand in the general direction of the Dalcerris' lake house. "These highfalutin' city folks think they can come up here whenever they feel like it and party all night long, carrying on and disturbing the peace. They think they're entitled just cause they've got money to burn—bringing all their friends, drinking and dancing on the beach like a pack of teenagers. They ought to be ashamed of themselves. I didn't get a wink of sleep all night."

Palmer raised a brow in a show of camaraderie. "I'm sorry to hear that, Larry. I can assure you that we take noise complaints very seriously. Was their music too loud?"

He tried to suppress a grin as he watched Larry struggle to maintain his composure. "I didn't say nothing about any music," he sputtered. "It was them laughing and hollering all night long that kept me up."

"An officer was dispatched to talk to them last night, so I can confirm that it's been taken care of."

Larry snorted and rubbed a grimy finger beneath his nose. "I'll believe that when I see it. They'll be right back at it next weekend."

"You're well within your rights to call again any time if they don't quiet down by 10:00 p.m.," Palmer said. "But my partner and I are actually here on another issue. You might have noticed all the activity on the beach this morning?"

Larry frowned, glancing over at the small window dotted with dead flies above the sink. "I haven't been outside, yet. Can't see much of anything from up here with all the trees. I like it better that way. No one spying on me, no one nosing around in my business."

"A young woman's body was recovered from the water this morning," Palmer said in a somber tone. He watched as something shifted in Larry's eyes, like an animal suddenly alerted to danger.

He jutted out his jaw. "What's that got to do with me?"

Palmer gave a polite cough as he flicked open his notebook. Of all the responses he'd anticipated, that wasn't one of them. Innocent people typically reacted with a mixture of shock and empathy. Clearly, Larry's thoughts were all about himself—a sociopathic tendency if ever there was one. No wonder Maria disliked him. He made no effort to connect with anyone, not even over a tragedy in his own back yard.

"We're conducting interviews with all the neighbors, as a matter of course," Palmer continued in a professional tone. "Did you happen to see or hear anything suspicious last night, other than your neighbors partying?"

Larry reached for a stained mug on the cracked tile counter and raised it to his lips, all the while staring over the rim at Palmer. "I never went outside. I heard them through the window."

"Did it sound like any of them were arguing or fighting?"

Larry wet his lips. "They might have been, come to think of it. I couldn't make out what they were saying."

Palmer raised his brows discreetly at Lopez. He wasn't getting a warm and cozy feeling from Larry's sly responses. But that in itself proved nothing. He cast a slow, deliberate gaze around the space, not detecting a woman's touch in the bleak color scheme. "Do you live alone, Larry?"

His trenched face hardened. "I do now."

Palmer raised a questioning brow. "Divorced?"

Larry gave a disgruntled nod.

Palmer made a note to himself to look into Larry's immediate family but decided not to delve any deeper into the touchy topic at present. He was more interested in finding out about the dead woman, and he needed to keep Larry talking. He pulled out his phone and scrolled through to the photo of the corpse. "Would you mind taking a look at this picture and letting me know if you recognize the woman?" He set his phone on the table and gestured to Larry to take a look.

Larry eyed Officer Lopez warily before lumbering over to where Palmer was seated. He reached for the phone with grubby fingers and scowled at the screen. Palmer masked his revulsion and made a mental note to disinfect his phone the minute he got home.

He watched as Larry drew his unruly brows together, working his jaw back-and-forth in the off-putting manner he had. Without a word, he tossed the phone on the table and shuffled off across the kitchen. He emptied the contents of his mug in the sink and scrambled around on the counter for something, his back toward Palmer. Instinctively, Palmer reached for his gun, but then he heard the click of a lighter. A moment later, cigarette smoke lofted through the air. Slowly, Larry turned back around to face him. He took several drags of his cigarette before he spoke. "I might've seen her. But I didn't do nothing to her."

Palmer's pulse quickened. He nodded encouragingly. "Go on."

Larry's gaze shifted restlessly between Palmer and Lopez. "They sent you here, didn't they? They said I had something to do with it." He sucked in a heavy breath, waving a nicotine-stained finger at them. "They're guilty as sin, mark my words. They're gonna try and pin this on me. Rich folks are all the same. They'll get some highfalutin' lawyer and pay him off—"

"You said you might have seen her before," Palmer interrupted. "Do you remember where?"

Larry sniffed and dragged a sleeve across his mouth. "She showed up at my door a couple of months back, asked if this was the Dalcerri household." He laughed, bending over as a cough ripped its way up his throat. "'No, this is the governor's mansion,' I said. She didn't think that was funny."

Palmer stretched a polite smile across his face. "Did she tell you her name?"

"No, and I didn't ask. Don't care to know."

"Did you notice what type of vehicle she was driving?"

"She pulled up in a black suburban, but she wasn't driving. She had some guy with her—gangster-looking type."

"Did you direct her to the Dalcerris?" Palmer asked.

Larry let out a humph. "Yeah, I did—wanted her off my property."

"Did she tell you what business she had with them?"

"I don't care to know other people's business," Larry retorted. "I figured she must've been looking for Alex. He was up here that weekend. His wife doesn't come up much. Anyway, she must have got ahold of him. It was almost an hour later before the black suburban came back down the road."

Palmer exchanged a glance with Lopez, before turning back to Larry. "How do you know that?"

"I was out on the front porch on my deck chair. I saw it go by. Souped up engine like a drug dealer drives." He took another puff of his cigarette and then stubbed it out in the sink. "Alex is up to no good. I seen that black suburban come and go on the road a few times since. I'm willing to bet his wife doesn't know nothing about it." He yanked open the drawer behind him and rummaged around in it, finally producing a dog-eared notebook. "I wrote down the license plate, just in case. I don't like suspicious characters trespassing on my property." He held out the notebook and Palmer took it and copied down the number.

"I'll look into it," Palmer said, getting to his feet. "Thanks for your help. It's always good to have a vigilant neighbor."

Larry sneered. "I think you mean vigilante."

10

"Larry Thompson's definitely a disturbing individual," Palmer muttered, as he and Lopez made their way outside.

Lopez grunted in agreement. "But is he dangerous?"

Palmer squared his shoulders. "That's what we need to find out."

Back in the squad car, he radioed the license plate Larry had given him into the station for a trace. Within minutes, he had a name and address. "Levi Hendrik," the officer on duty told him. "He has a record. He's a known drug dealer and petty criminal."

Palmer hung up and grimaced at Lopez. "Sounds like Larry was right about the shady company Alex Dalcerri keeps. Makes you wonder if that nutritional supplement business his wife runs is a front for something else."

Lopez nodded thoughtfully. "Either that, or she has no clue what her husband gets up to when he's at their lake house supposedly working on his thriller novels."

"We'll bring him in for questioning," Palmer said. "He knows who the dead woman is. I saw it written all over his face. He's terrified that whatever secret he's hiding is going to come out."

"What about the wife?" Lopez asked. "Do you think she's complicit?"

"Hard to say. She does a good job of keeping her emotions in check. But she calls the shots in that relationship. I'm pretty sure she'll lawyer up the minute we tell her we want to talk to her husband." Palmer drummed his fingers on the dash for a moment. "I have a nagging feeling that Alex Dalcerri is mixed up with the dead woman, and Brock Wagner knows something about it. He was very distraught when we arrived on the scene, and evasive when we showed him the dead woman's photo. I'm willing to bet he recognized her too. I want to pay him and his wife a visit at their home—see if he opens up once Alex isn't around to make sure he keeps his mouth shut."

Palmer's phone rang and he pressed it to his ear. "Hey Jack. Got anything more for me?"

"I'm afraid not," the ME replied. "We've done all we can on site. Just wanted to let you know that we're taking the body back to the lab now. I'll have my full report on your desk in the next day or two."

"All right. Keep me posted." Palmer hung up and started the engine. He backed up carefully as he looked for a spot to turn around without puncturing a tire on any rusted implements hidden from view in Larry's overgrown yard. "We can release the Dalcerris' guests now that the crime scene's been processed," he said to Lopez. "Make sure you have all their contact info before they leave. Once they're out of here, we'll ask the Dalcerris to come down to the local station to sign a statement. I'll hit Alex up with the information Larry gave us and see what he has to say about it. We'll interview Maria separately —try and find out what she knows, if anything."

The other couples looked visibly relieved when Palmer relayed the news that they were free to go. "We'll follow up with you in the next day or two once we hear from the medical examiner," Palmer said.

They wasted no time grabbing their belongings and bidding Maria and Alex a subdued goodbye. For her part, Maria was vocal in her apologies for the shocking turn the weekend had taken.

"You have nothing to apologize for. It's not your fault," Ivy assured her. "Please call me if there's anything we can do."

Alex remained stone-faced as the departing guests exchanged awkward hugs and handshakes before heading out to their vehicles.

"I'm going to ask the two of you to come down to the local sheriff's station and give a statement," Palmer said, as the sound of cars crunching down the gravel driveway faded from earshot.

"What?" Alex turned to him, a look of shock detonating in his face. "Why? We already told you everything we know."

"The body was discovered at your dock. As the homeowners, I need to take your statements and have you sign them—just following procedure, that's all," Palmer replied calmly.

"How long is this going to take?" Maria asked, frowning at her Apple Watch.

"Not long," Palmer assured her.

Maria sighed. "Fine. I'll get changed and grab my purse."

Alex suppressed a scowl and followed her out of the kitchen.

Palmer exchanged a knowing look with Lopez. "I have a sneaking suspicion things are about to get very interesting."

HALF AN HOUR LATER, Palmer and Lopez took their seats opposite Alex Dalcerri in the only interview room the station had to offer—a stuffy, windowless box that sorely lacked the lake breeze Alex enjoyed at his writing desk.

Palmer flipped opened his notebook. "Tell me again from the beginning exactly what happened this morning."

"I can't add anything to what I've already told you," Alex said in a snippy tone. "I was asleep when Maria woke me up. She was all freaked out—said there was an elderly woman in the kitchen who thought she'd seen a body in the water. She told me to go check it out." He rubbed a hand over his jaw, glancing warily between Palmer and Lopez. "I never thought for a minute it would actually turn out to be a body. I went down to the water with Brock and that's when we found her in the pondweed."

Palmer made a point of consulting his notes. "And you stated that neither you nor Brock Wagner recognized the woman?"

Alex cleared his throat. "That's correct."

Palmer let a moment's silence unwind as he observed Alex rubbing the palm of his hand up and down the leg of his pants in an agitated fashion. Palmer placed his phone on the table between them. "Take all the time you need to consider your answer. Are you sure you don't recognize this woman?"

Alex swallowed and pushed the phone back toward Palmer with an air of revulsion. "Is this really necessary? How many times have I told you already, I don't know her?"

"And yet you met her at your home, isn't that right, Alex? Several times, in fact."

Palmer was fascinated at how quickly the color drained from the man's face. His lips parted briefly and then smashed together as if deciding against divulging whatever it was he'd been about to say. "I don't know what you're talking about. If we're done here, I have somewhere else I need to be." Without waiting for a response, he shoved his chair out from the table and stood.

Palmer motioned for him to sit back down. "We won't be much longer. I just need to straighten out a couple more things before you leave. I'm going to need the dead woman's name, and also the name of the man who drove the black suburban that was seen at your lake house several times in the past few months."

Alex passed a shaking hand over his forehead. "Who ... who told you that?"

"A confidential source," Palmer replied, looking him square in the eye. "Do you want to cooperate or not? We can do this the easy way or the hard way."

Alex sank back down in his seat, a shell-shocked expression settling in the grooves beneath his eyes. He ran trembling fingers over his jaw and then crossed his arms in front of him in a bid to keep them from shaking. "All right, I admit I met her a few times. But I had nothing to do with what happened to her, you have to believe me." Unfolding his arms, he placed his palms on the table, and leaned forward with a pleading expression in his eyes. "You can't tell Maria about this, whatever you do."

Palmer eyed him gravely. "You're not really in a position to make those kinds of demands. If you were having an affair, I won't make it my business to break it to your wife. But if either of you were involved in this woman's death, you'd better believe I'm going to make it my business to find out."

"I wasn't having an affair with her," Alex spat back. "I swear to you. I've never been unfaithful to my wife."

"Go on," Palmer said sternly.

Alex's shoulders sank and his eyes glazed over as if he were trying to gather his thoughts. "Her name's Tay Nicholson—at least, that's what she told me. I don't know the guy she worked for—Levi something or other. He's a loan shark. I needed money, and I didn't want Maria to know about it."

Palmer tried to mask his surprise at the direction the confession had taken. He'd been expecting Alex to admit to having an affair with the woman. Lonely writer meets woman half his age who's enamored by the romantic notion of dating a thriller author. The loan shark angle was a twist Palmer hadn't seen coming. Not from a man who appeared to be very comfortably off. Still, appearances could be deceptive. Palmer leaned back in his chair and observed Alex. "What did you need the money for?"

He squirmed in his seat. "It's irrelevant—just some bills I had to take care of. The point is, I didn't do anything to Tay. It's the guy she worked for you should be talking to. He's a thug. He probably bumped her off and needed a place to dump the body. He knew this area from coming up here to collect his money."

"An intriguing theory," Palmer said dismissively. "But I'm more interested in talking about you. When was the last time you saw Tay Nicholson?"

"Last weekend," Alex answered, without any hesitation. He seemed eager to talk now that Palmer had called him out on his lies. "She stopped by briefly to collect a payment on the loan. That's how they did it. She came to the door, and he stayed in the car."

Palmer jotted down a few notes, trying to keep his skepticism from showing. "How did you find this loan shark to begin with?"

Alex flushed, averting his eyes. "Some online ad. Like I said, I had to keep things discreet. I could have asked Maria for the money, but I didn't want her finding out why I needed it."

Palmer tapped the end of his pen on the table in an irritated fashion. He was fairly certain Alex was still lying to him. "I'm going to need you to come clean about why you needed the money so I can verify what you're telling me."

Alex scratched his jaw in an agitated manner. "My cousin lost his job and fell behind on a few months of mortgage payments. He asked me to help him out. Maria was never too fond of helping out my family. Please, don't mention it to her."

Palmer cocked a disbelieving brow at him. "I'll need your cousin's number."

Alex reached for the pen and paper Palmer passed across the table and dutifully wrote down some information.

Palmer had the distinct feeling it wouldn't pan out. Alex had likely changed a digit to buy himself some time to talk his cousin into corroborating his story—if he even had a cousin.

Alex Dalcerri was hiding a lot more than he was admitting to. If he had anything to do with Tay Nicholson's watery demise, Palmer would get to the bottom of it.

11

Ensconced in a plastic chair in the reception seating area in the police station, Maria pulled out her phone to tackle her backlog of emails while she waited on Alex. She wasn't sure why Palmer thought it necessary to take their statements separately, but he'd assured her it was standard procedure, and she had complied—eager to do her part to assist in the investigation. It was a terrible thing that had happened, and most unfortunate that the woman's body had drifted to their dock. Maria suspected it would turn out to be another intoxicated young person who had walked out onto the shared subdivision dock late at night and fallen in. She might have had a row with a boyfriend. Hopefully, someone would come forward soon with information. It was an awful tragedy, all the way around.

With a stoic sigh, she set about responding to a few pressing business matters. She would have to reschedule the celebratory weekend with Ricki and Ivy—a different venue would be in order, in light of what had happened. She was eager to tell them the news that her lawyer was in the process of drawing up the paperwork for the stock option she'd promised them, but it seemed an inappropriate time to bring it up now.

After responding to a few texts, she opened up an email from her accountant, Damien, requesting her to look over the attached spreadsheets, and give him a call, as soon as possible. She creased her brow in frustration—she'd already checked the numbers carefully before she'd forwarded him the financials to prepare her taxes. After peering down the corridor for any sign of Detective Palmer and her husband, she opened up the first spreadsheet and began perusing the figures. Damien had highlighted several line entries and added a comment by each one. Maria scratched her forehead as she read through them. It appeared he had some concerns that there was money missing from the company's accounts—including a couple of fairly large amounts. All in all, they were off by close to $600,000. She frowned as she smoothed her hair back from her face and dialed Damien's number. It had to be a clerical error.

"Hey, it's the weekend, you're not supposed to be working," Damien answered.

"Neither are you, but you sent me an email."

"I figured you wouldn't get around to looking at it until Monday. I thought you were going up to the lake to celebrate with Ricki and Ivy this weekend."

"Yeah, it didn't pan out quite the way I'd hoped." Maria hesitated. She didn't want to get into what had happened with Damien on the phone. "I'll fill you in some other time. About your email—it's probably an honest mistake by my CFO. I can have her look into it on Monday."

"I already talked to her on Friday to get some clarification," Damien replied. "She was adamant those line entries weren't hers. I hate to break it to you, Maria, but it looks like someone in your office dummied up a bunch of invoices. Whoever it was, they didn't do a great job of covering their tracks."

Maria clutched the phone tighter in her fist, digesting the news. How was that possible? Apart from her CFO, the only other person with administrative access to the *XCellNourish* accounts was Alex. A sick feeling swirled inside her gut. Did this have something to do with the antidepressants?

"We're ready for you now," Lopez called to her from the hallway.

Startled, she hurriedly ended the call with Damien. "Gotta run. I'll figure it out and call you back later."

"Where's Alex?" Maria asked, as she followed Lopez into a bleak-looking interview room, befitting her plummeting mood. She eyed the hard plastic chair Lopez gestured toward with distaste. She dreaded to think of all the drunks and drifters who occupied the chairs on the weekends. She was trusting they disinfected them on a regular basis. Gingerly, she slid her purse onto the table in front of her.

"Your husband's reviewing his statement before he signs it," Lopez explained. "He'll be waiting for you in the lobby when you're done."

The door swung open, and Palmer breezed in. "Sorry to keep you waiting," he announced. He plonked down on the seat next to Lopez and pulled out a black notebook.

"I hope this isn't going to take long," Maria said, crossing her legs. "It turns out, I have a pressing business matter I need to attend to."

"Understood. I appreciate your patience," Palmer responded gravely.

Maria frowned at the noncommittal answer. She was beginning to wonder if she should have called her lawyer before agreeing to this. Alex had been in with the detectives for over an hour. Surely, it couldn't take that long to repeat what he'd already told them at the house. It wasn't that Maria was opposed to helping with the investigation, but the accounting discrepancy at the office took precedence now. She needed to wrap this up, as quickly as possible, and get back down to Masonville Springs to sort things out.

Palmer scrolled through his phone for a moment or two, and then placed it on the table in front of her. "I'd like you to take another look at this photo and think very carefully before you give me an answer. Have you ever seen this woman before?"

An uneasy feeling tugged in the pit of Maria's stomach. *Think very carefully.* Was he cautioning her? And why was Palmer going over the same questions again? Isn't that what the police did to suspects, hoping to trip them up? She was only supposed to be here to give her statement. Resigning herself to getting it over with, she pulled the phone closer and peered at the lifeless face once more. She couldn't afford to make a mistake in a murder investigation. In her mind, she ran through her social circles and business associates. The young woman wasn't an employee, that much she was certain of. Was it possible she'd met her on some other occasion? Perhaps she was a girlfriend of one of her employees, or a vendor's family member. After racking her brain, she shook her head. "No, I don't recognize her."

Palmer stroked his chin, studying her thoughtfully. "What would you say if I told you that your husband has admitted to knowing her?"

Maria's mouth dropped open, her eyes zigzagging between Palmer and Lopez. "I ... I don't understand. What are you talking about? Alex said he didn't recognize her."

"He was lying earlier," Palmer answered. "Her name's Tay Nicholson. He met with her multiple times over the past few months at your lake house."

Maria pressed a hand to her neck, the acid in her stomach churning like the lake in a storm, as the detective's words sank in. Alex *knew* the dead woman and had *lied* about it. They'd been meeting behind her back for months. Was he having an affair? She'd never suspected a thing, but it certainly explained why he was making virtually no progress on his novel all those weekends when he claimed to be hard at work. Indignation rose inside her, rage and shame washing over her in equal parts. "Are you sure it was the dead woman?"

"I'm afraid so," Palmer confirmed. "We have a witness who saw her coming and going. I take it you were in the dark about this?"

Maria nodded numbly, a chill spreading through her bones. The room seemed to be closing in on her. What had started out as a tragedy she'd been emotionally detached from, had suddenly turned into something intensely personal. She cleared her throat and choked out the words, "I had no idea Alex was ... having an affair."

Palmer studied her with a keen eye. "Interestingly, he denies having an affair with the woman. He claims he borrowed money from a loan shark she worked for and was paying it back in installments. He wouldn't say why he needed the money, at first. He finally disclosed that he was helping a cousin of his who'd fallen behind with his mortgage payments. He says he didn't ask you for the money because he didn't want you knowing he was helping out his family."

Maria rubbed her forehead, confusion clouding her thoughts. Who could Alex be helping? She'd never even met his cousins—both of whom lived in Australia. "I don't understand. Why would he need to borrow money from a loan shark? He could have come to me. I would have—"

She broke off as it hit her like a thunderbolt. *The missing money!* He'd already helped himself. There was no question in her mind that it was Alex who'd stolen the money from the company. But why had he taken it? The amount that was missing far exceeded a few months of mortgage payments.

"You were saying?" Palmer prompted.

Maria swatted the space between them. "Nothing. I was just thinking out loud. I'm confused right now."

In fact, she was thinking about the prescription pills she'd discovered in Alex's shaving bag and wondering if they had anything to do with the missing money—not a connection she was eager to divulge to Detective Palmer. The more she thought about it, the more it made sense. Alex had been acting strangely of late, distancing himself from her. He claimed he'd been taking antidepressants because his writing wasn't going well. But he wouldn't need the kind of money that was missing from *XCellNourish's* accounts to purchase them. She couldn't help wondering if he was peddling drugs. It would explain why he'd hidden the pills from her. But how deep of a mess was he really in? Her heart sank. If the media got even a whiff of this, it would destroy everything she'd worked so hard to build.

12

After wrapping up the interviews with Alex and Maria, Palmer and Lopez had headed back down the mountain to Masonville Springs. It was only an hour's drive, which made it an easy commute for city folks heading to the lake to escape the heat of summer.

Back at the station, Palmer had retired to his office to try and track down Tay Nicholson's next-of-kin, in the hope of securing a positive identification. He'd discovered she was unmarried and the only daughter of a drug-addicted mother whose whereabouts were currently unknown. Through DMV records, he'd identified Tay's current address and obtained a warrant to search her apartment.

He glanced up when Lopez appeared in the doorway. "What do you think, boss? Did the thriller writer do it?"

Palmer rubbed a hand over his brow. "Hard to say. Money does strange things to people. If the Nicholson woman showed up to collect a payment, and an argument broke out, it's entirely possible. But we don't have any evidence to hold him."

"Maybe the wife knows something and she's covering for him," Lopez suggested, sinking down in the chair opposite Palmer.

Palmer frowned. "If she is, she's a smooth liar, I'll give her that."

He cracked his knuckles before reaching for his lukewarm coffee. "There are a lot of layers to this case. At this point, it's anyone's guess who all's involved. I'm still not ruling out the idea that Tay was at that party at the Dalcerris' lake house."

Lopez interlaced his hands behind his head and gazed up at the ceiling. "We can't rule out that dark horse, Larry Thompson either. That vigilante comment he made was bizarre—maybe he was livid enough about the racket they were making next door to do one of them in."

Palmer drained his coffee and tossed the cup in the trash. "Like I said, lots of layers. All I know for certain is that Alex is lying about what he needed the money for, and Maria keeps her cards close to her chest. Ready to roll? Maybe we'll find the evidence we need to crack this case wide open at Tay Nicholson's apartment."

A desk sergeant stuck her head around the door. "I emailed you that background check on Larry Thompson, a few minutes ago."

"Great. I'll look it over before I leave." Palmer reached for his keyboard and opened up the email, glancing briefly through the attached document. "He has a record. Can't say I'm surprised. It says here his wife, Sheila Thompson, filed domestic abuse charges against him in 2007."

"Did he do any time?" Lopez asked.

"No. She ended up dropping the charges and divorcing him." Palmer frowned as he scrolled through the remainder of the report. "The cops were called out to their house on three other occasions during the course of their marriage, but she never pursued charges."

Lopez grunted in disgust. "So we know he has violent tendencies. Looks like we have ourselves another suspect. Do we have an address for the ex?"

"Yes. Home and work," Palmer confirmed. "We'll pay her a visit after we're done at the Nicholson place. CSI said they could meet us there at 4:00 p.m. We'd better head that way."

Tay Nicholson's place was on the ground floor of a crumbling apartment block painted a sad-looking uniform gray on the east side of town. Palmer and Lopez made their way to the manager's office and showed her their search warrant.

She crumpled her face in displeasure before disappearing into the back office to fetch a key. "She's in 201. She's never given me any trouble before," she announced when she remerged. "What did she do, anyway?"

"She's deceased," Palmer explained.

The manager's scowl morphed into shock. "Tay's *dead*? What happened to her?"

"We're still investigating the circumstances surrounding her death. Do you have an emergency contact number for her in your files?"

The woman frowned and turned to her computer screen. She tapped on a grubby-looking keyboard, for several minutes, and then peeled a Post-it note from a pad next to the phone. After scribbling something down, she handed the note to Palmer. "She listed her boss as her emergency contact. That's his number."

Palmer thanked her and accompanied Lopez out of the office and across the courtyard to Tay's apartment.

At first glance, 201 appeared to be a relatively organized space with no obvious signs that anything untoward had occurred inside its walls. CSI would go over it with a fine-tooth comb, nonetheless, once they arrived on scene. Pulling on his gloves, Palmer began leafing through some paperwork on the kitchen counter—bills, circulars, a reminder card for an upcoming dental appointment, and a women's magazine Tay subscribed to.

His gaze drifted to a small black velvet box next to the toaster. He picked it up and opened it, surprised to find a large, diamond ring nesting inside. He was no expert on jewelry, but he guessed it was worth a considerable amount of money. It seemed strange that a woman would leave a valuable ring like this sitting out in plain sight. Why was it in a box and not on her finger? Maybe she was taking it to be cleaned.

Lopez peered over his shoulder at the ring and let out a low whistle. "That's a beauty. At least a carat, I reckon."

"What I want to know is, why is it sitting on the kitchen counter?" Palmer said. "Wouldn't most women either wear it, or keep it locked up in their jewelry box, or a safe even?"

Lopez nodded thoughtfully. "Something about it doesn't feel right. What if she decided to call off an engagement? Maybe that's why she ended up dead."

"Do you think the fiancé could be this Levi Hendrick guy—her so-called boss?"

Lopez gave a baffled shake of his head. "Let's hope not. If he's running an illegal loan shark operation, I'm betting he knows how to get rid of people."

"Apparently, not how to hide a body very well." Palmer flattened his lips in a grimace. "He's definitely another person of interest. We'll pay him a visit. Our pool of suspects keeps growing."

He moved into the only bedroom in the apartment and did a cursory search of the space. To his surprise, he discovered a cell phone charging in an outlet under the bed. "That's odd. Who leaves the house without their phone these days?"

"No one—not voluntarily," Lopez said.

"Bag it up for now," Palmer replied. "We'll have the tech team unlock it."

He looked up at the sound of footsteps thudding down the hallway. A CSI tech poked a hair-netted head inside. "Ready for us?"

Palmer gave a brisk nod. "All yours. Call me if you find anything."

LARRY'S EX-WIFE, Sheila, was standing in her front yard smoking a cigarette and talking to her neighbor over the fence, when Palmer and Lopez pulled up outside her modular home in a less than desirable neighborhood on the other side of town. Dressed in a sleeveless T-shirt and an unflattering pair of frayed, cut-off shorts, her face bore the haggard crevices of a chain smoker. Her hooded eyes narrowed as they approached.

"Are you Sheila Thompson?" Palmer asked.

She took a puff of her cigarette, giving them a leisurely once over. "Who's asking?"

Palmer flashed his ID and introduced himself and Lopez. "We have a few questions about your ex-husband, Larry Thompson."

She raised an overly plucked brow. "What's he gone and done now?"

Palmer threw a pointed look at her neighbor who was listening in on the conversation with unabashed curiosity. "I'd prefer to discuss it inside. May we come in?"

Sheila shrugged and gestured to the open door. "Talk later, Babs," she said to her neighbor, before tossing her cigarette on the gravel driveway and smashing it beneath her cracked flip-flop.

Palmer cast a keen glance around the kitchen she led them into. Evidently Larry and Sheila shared a lack of housekeeping standards, if nothing else. Palmer wrinkled his nose at the odor of stale cigarettes and mold that hung in the air. Dirty dishes filled the sink, and the counter space was cluttered with miscellaneous items. An overflowing plastic laundry basket sat atop the table. Sheila reached for it and promptly dropped it in a corner of the room. "The washer's broken—again. It's a pain lugging stuff to the laundromat."

Palmer flashed her a polite smile.

"All right, hit me with it. What's Larry got himself into?" Sheila prodded, flopping down at the kitchen table and folding her arms in front of her.

"A young woman's body was recovered at the lake this weekend," Palmer explained. "We're interviewing everyone as a matter of course. The body was found in the pondweed close to Larry's next-door neighbors' dock."

Sheila's eyes bulged as she blew air in and out of her cheeks. After a moment, her lips split in a cunning smile. "You're wondering if he did it, aren't you? You think he killed her." She slid down in her seat with a satisfied gleam in her eyes, waiting for Palmer to confirm the brilliance of her theory.

"It may have been an accidental drowning. We're not sure of the cause of death, yet," he responded, careful to keep his tone impassive.

"I understand you filed domestic abuse charges against your ex-husband back in 2007. Why did you drop those charges?"

A flicker of unease crossed Sheila's face. "Don't go putting this on me. It's not my fault if he finally went out and did someone in. I got out when I could, the best way I knew how. Trust me, I knew better than to rattle his cage." She picked at the skin on her finger, staring morosely at her discolored nails for several minutes. "He threatened to carve my face up like a turkey if I didn't drop the charges."

"Do you believe he's capable of that kind of violence?" Palmer asked.

Sheila locked eyes with him, slowly raising her shirt to expose a web of raised scars across her belly.

13

No one answered the door at Levi Hendrix's address in another disreputable downtown neighborhood. Palmer surveyed the street, fully aware of the suspicious glances being directed his way by several young males loitering in a nearby alleyway. He jammed a business card into the splintered door frame and strode back to the squad car where Lopez was waiting for him. "No joy," he said, as Lopez started up the car.

"No sign of the black suburban either. Let's head back to the station and go over what we've gathered so far."

Back in his office, Palmer pulled up his case notes on the computer and reviewed them with Lopez. "Background checks on the Dalcerris, Wagners, and O'Shaughnessys are in. Apart from a couple of speeding tickets, the Dalcerris and Wagners are clean. Jim O'Shaughnessy was cited for threatening a police officer at his daughter's funeral. There was an ongoing investigation into her death at the time, so he was shown some leniency. Several of the mourners also reported overhearing him threatening to kill the person he blamed for spiking his daughter's drink."

"It wouldn't surprise me if O'Shaughnessy has swung a few

punches in his day," Lopez remarked. "He was ready to clock you at the lake house. I was close to dangling my handcuffs in his face."

"He's a hothead, no doubt about it," Palmer concurred. "His wife says he's still consumed by his daughter's death. I found a picture of her in the case file." He turned the screen to face Lopez. "Beautiful girl."

"Yeah, she was a looker, all right," Lopez agreed. "What does the police report on the accident say?"

"The autopsy determined she had alcohol and fentanyl in her system," Palmer replied. "She stepped right out in front of a car, high as a kite. The driver had no chance to swerve. She was only twenty-three years old. Every father's nightmare."

Lopez shook his head. "That would mess you up in a big way."

A member of the tech team knocked and entered the office. "Here's that phone you wanted unlocked," he said, setting an evidence bag containing Tay's phone on the desk.

"That was quick," Palmer said, with a note of appreciation in his voice.

"Nothing to it if you know what you're doing," the young officer with a sprig of ginger on his chin replied, with a smirk.

Palmer and Lopez exchanged a knowing look as he exited the room with heightened swagger.

"Oh to be young and invincible again," Palmer groaned, reaching for the bagged phone. "Now, let's see what kind of relationship Tay Nicholson really had with Levi Hendrix."

"Fifty bucks he was the fiancé," Lopez said. "My guess is she was trying to break it off with him and he did her in."

"Then why leave the engagement ring behind?" Palmer asked. "He must have seen it. It was sitting out in plain view on the counter."

Lopez shrugged. "You got me there."

Palmer opened up the Gmail app on Tay's phone and glanced through her emails. Judging by the quantity of sales and marketing pitches clogging her inbox, she reveled in an excessive amount of online shopping. Evidently, business was good, whatever that entailed—most likely, a cut of the loans she procured for Levi. Palmer couldn't find any communication at all on her phone from Levi. Maybe he went by some other name to keep his disreputable business ventures under wraps.

There was an email from the Apple store confirming Tay's appointment at the Genius Bar, and one from her bank notifying her that her credit card payment was due. Everything else was promotions, receipts, or spam of one kind or another. He checked Tay's text messages next and zeroed in on a thread from someone identified only as *Governor* with an intimidating-looking military avatar. It had to be Levi. The thread was mostly confirming customer pickup locations and times. "Sounds like she and Levi conducted a lot of business together," Palmer mused. "But there's nothing here to indicate they were romantically involved."

Lopez suppressed a yawn. "So now we're looking for someone else —a mysterious fiancé. What was that you were saying about a suspect pool that keeps on growing?"

Palmer ran a hand through his hair. "I'm not ruling out Levi as a suspect, yet. Maybe he discovered she was stealing from him and decided to make an example of her."

"Yeah, maybe," Lopez agreed, rubbing his eyes with the back of his hands.

Palmer eyed him appraisingly. "It's late. You should get out of here. Go hug your kids."

"What about you?" Lopez asked. "Don't you need to get home to Mrs. Palmer?"

"She's used to my irregular hours. Gives her a chance to binge all those Netflix shows I hate." Palmer made a shooing motion with his hand. "Go home while your kids are still young."

Lopez gave him a friendly salute as he exited the office. Palmer leaned back and stared blankly at the notes on his computer screen for a few more minutes, before getting to his feet and making his way to the coffee machine in the corridor. His thoughts gravitated to the lifeless body bobbing up and down in the pondweed at Tamarack Creek Lake. The contusion on Tay's head was a major red flag. If Jack determined the cause of death to be blunt force trauma, this would become a homicide investigation. Something in his gut told him the sooner he got to work assembling the evidence, the better.

Caffeine in hand, he made his way back to his office and picked up Tay's phone again. He made a few notes about a couple of her contacts he'd like to talk to, including Levi Hendrix. He still needed to rule out any romantic attachment between them.

Opening up Tay's photo app, he began scrolling languidly through it. Interestingly, there were several pictures of Tamarack Creek Lake, and even a couple of the Dalcerris' house, which confirmed Larry's contention that Tay had been there, on at least one occasion. Most of the photo stream consisted of staged selfies of Tay in clubs or restaurants—living the high life. He continued flicking through the pictures aimlessly, reversing course when he spotted one of Tay sporting an engagement ring. He enlarged the photo and studied it from several angles. It appeared to be the same ring he'd found at her apartment. He sent a copy of the photo to himself to compare to the ring later. He had a hunch the diamond was somehow connected to Tay's death. If she had a fiancé, he was keeping a questionably low profile in the wake of her death.

After perusing several dozen banal photos of everything from sunsets to artfully arranged plates of food, he came to an abrupt halt at a photo of Tay in a bar, clutching a cocktail. A tingling feeling went down his spine. She was laughing into the camera as she and another woman angled their heads together for the shot. He'd seen that woman before.

It was the O'Shaughnessys' daughter.

14

vy was just about to sit down to a late breakfast after a sleepless night when the doorbell rang. "How's that for timing?" she groaned.

"Want me to get it?" Jim asked gruffly, as he doused his plate of scrambled eggs with ketchup.

"No, I'll get it. It's probably just Teri next door. She promised to drop off a magazine for me." Ivy tightened the belt on her bathrobe as she shuffled to the front door in her sheepskin slippers. Opening it, she raised her brows in confusion at the sight of Palmer and Lopez standing on the doorstep. "Oh, I didn't expect—" Her voice trailed off. She remembered that they'd mentioned they would be following up with them back in Masonville Springs. Maybe they had an update on how the young woman had died.

"Can we come in for a few minutes?" Palmer asked, tilting his hat at her.

"Yes, of course." Ivy gestured them inside and closed the front door behind them. "Go straight ahead into the kitchen. Jim and I were just sitting down to eat breakfast. We didn't get much sleep last night." She hesitated before adding, "This whole situation has brought back a lot of difficult memories for us. My husband's not coping well. I have to warn you, his temper can still flare up quickly."

"I understand. This won't take long," Palmer assured her.

The expression on Jim's face darkened the minute the two officers walked into his field of view. He shoved a forkful of food into his mouth and chewed loudly, glaring at them.

Ivy groaned inwardly. Did he have to make a point of signaling how much he despised them at every opportunity?

"Please, take a seat," she said to the officers, before sitting down in front of her plate of untouched food. "Have there been any developments?"

"We've identified the deceased woman as Tay Nicholson," Palmer replied.

Ivy pressed her fingertips to her forehead, silently repeating the name. It didn't ring a bell, which was a relief. She would hate for it to have been someone they knew, even in passing. "It's so sad for her family. I take it you've already notified them, if you're releasing her name to the public?"

Palmer squared his jaw. "She has no immediate family, other than her mother who's an addict with no fixed abode. We're in the process of trying to track down her fiancé."

Ivy flinched. "Oh no! Poor guy. I can't imagine getting the news that your fiancée has drowned."

"No one said she drowned," Jim cut in, wiping his lips on a napkin. "Maybe the fiancé bumped her off."

"Jim!" Ivy threw him a horrified look. "Have some respect."

He shrugged. "Happens all the time."

"Does the name Tay Nicholson mean anything to either of you?" Palmer asked.

"No, I'm afraid not," Ivy answered.

Palmer looked pointedly at Jim who flapped an irritated hand in his direction. "I've already told you I don't know who she is. I've never set eyes on her before. Now, if you don't mind, we're trying to enjoy our breakfast."

"They're just doing their job, Jim," Ivy protested.

"Doing their job," he echoed, his voice elevating to an all-too-familiar pitch. "Is that what you call interrupting us on Sunday morning with lame questions we've already answered?" He heaped his fork with scrambled egg and shoved it into his mouth.

Ivy threw him a remonstrative look. If he kept this up, it wouldn't be long before he'd be handcuffed and dragged out to the squad car. A shudder ran through her at the thought. He'd come close to assaulting a police officer before. He'd threatened him after Emily's death, accused him of sitting on his hands and doing nothing. But what more could the police have done? Toxicology reports had shown that Emily was high on fentanyl. Jim remained convinced that someone had slipped it into her drink, but there was no way to prove it. As agonizing as it was at the time, they had been left with no choice but to bury their daughter and move on without the answers they so desperately wanted.

"I'd like you both to take a look at another photo for me," Palmer said in a measured tone. "I need to warn you that this might be painful."

"We're not interested in looking at that dead woman again," Jim growled. "You've put us through enough already."

"Actually, it's a photo of two young women in a bar. One of them is Tay Nicholson." Palmer hesitated, his tone softening. "I believe the other woman is your daughter, Emily. It's time-stamped the day she passed away."

The color drained from Jim's face as the fork slipped from his fingers and clattered to the floor. Ivy dug her nails into the palms of her hands, watching clots of scrambled egg go flying across the floor in slow motion. Her legs shook beneath the table as Palmer's words reverberated around inside her head. She tried to force herself to think rationally. It couldn't be Emily. Palmer must be mistaken. Why would Emily be in a photo with the woman who'd been found floating in Tamarack Creek Lake?

"Let me see that," Jim demanded, a guarded look in his eyes.

Palmer scrolled on his phone for a moment or two and then passed it to Jim. Ivy jumped up and hurried around to the other side of the table to join him. She gasped when she caught sight of her daughter sitting in an upscale bar, cocktail in hand, smiling blithely into the camera. Her head was angled in close to a blonde woman who looked uncannily like the dead girl, except her hair had been dark.

Ivy's head spun as she tried in vain to make sense of what she was seeing. Her heart was fluttering so fast in her chest she was half-afraid she was going to have a heart attack. She threw Jim an alarmed look. He was staring fixedly at the phone screen, a hard cord pulsing in his neck. For the past few months, he'd been consumed with hatred for the unidentified person he blamed for spiking Emily's drink. At her funeral, he'd sworn to tear the stranger limb from limb if he ever got his hands on them.

Ivy lifted her gaze to find Palmer staring directly at her. She could read the unspoken question in his eyes—had Jim O'Shaughnessy avenged his daughter's death?

15

Ivy pulled up at the Eagle Summit Mall and parked under the shade of a maple tree. She took several deep breaths before climbing out and locking her car. As soon as Palmer and Lopez had left, she had called Ricki and Maria, and asked them to meet her for a late lunch. She hadn't wanted to say too much over the phone, but she desperately needed to unload her fears on someone. The truth was she wanted them to talk her down off the ledge and reassure her that she was worrying needlessly. It was ridiculous to think that Jim could have had anything to do with Tay's death. Her thoughts had bolted like a runaway train under the stress of the situation—seeing that photo of Emily and Tay together had thrown her for a loop. It had to be just a strange coincidence. Deep down, she knew it must be, but the nagging thought that there was more to it wouldn't leave her alone.

She was still toying with the idea that Jim might have hired a private investigator to track down the mysterious stranger in the bar, unbeknownst to her. She'd been dead set against the idea when he'd first floated it a week or two after the funeral. She'd wanted to mourn their beloved Emily in peace, savor the happy memories instead of chasing ghosts. Besides, the police had already exhausted every lead.

Even the bartender hadn't noticed anything untoward, or anyone harassing Emily that night. The authorities had concluded it was nothing more than a tragic accident.

Ivy squeezed the strap of her purse, a nerve twitching below her left eye as she entered the mall. After Palmer and Lopez had left the house, she'd confronted Jim. She'd wanted to make absolutely certain he hadn't known before today who Tay Nicholson was. He'd flown into a rage like she'd never seen before. Even now, her stomach twisted at the unsettling memory. He'd actually thrown his breakfast plate against the wall, then grabbed her by the arms and shaken her until her teeth knocked together, before storming out of the house. She knew it wasn't really her he'd wanted to lash out at, but it made her realize Jim was capable of violence, given the right circumstances, and it terrified her.

Lost in her thoughts, she wove through the bustling mall to the cafe where she'd arranged to meet Ricki and Maria. She moved woodenly through the jovial crowds, feeling like a discombobulated spirit weaving among the bodies of the passersby. She couldn't get the photo of Emily and Tay laughing together in the bar out of her head. What did it mean? Was it connected in any way to Tay's death?

"Are you all right?" Ricki asked, when Ivy sat down next to her at the table.

"You do look awfully pale," Maria added, eying her with concern. "I suppose you couldn't sleep either. I feel terrible about what happened at the lake. I know we're all traumatized from it." She laid a hand on Ivy's arm. "It must have been especially hard on you and Jim. That young woman looked to be about Emily's age."

Ivy reached for the water carafe on the table and hurriedly poured herself a drink. "It's worse, much worse than you know," she rasped, setting down her glass with a thunk.

Ricki blinked, looking uneasy. "What do you mean?"

Before Ivy had a chance to respond, the waitress showed up to take their order.

"Just water for me," Ivy said. "And some lemon, please."

"You have to eat something," Maria chided. "You look like you're about to pass out."

Ivy glanced distractedly at the menu. "Fine, I'll have a Chicken Caesar salad."

The waitress made a note of their orders and waltzed off.

Ivy let out a long, shuddering sigh. "Palmer and his sidekick paid us a visit this morning."

Maria raised alarmed brows. "Really? They haven't come by our place, yet. What did they want?"

"They've identified the dead woman. Her name's Tay Nicholson."

"Yes, Palmer informed me yesterday after you all left. I don't know her," Maria said, her eyes glazing over.

"Doesn't ring a bell with me either," Ricki said, chewing on her lip. "Do you know her or something?"

"*I* don't." Ivy lowered her voice. "But apparently Emily did. Palmer showed me a photo he found on Tay's phone of the two of them drinking together at a bar." Her voice broke as she fought to hold back tears. "It was taken the night Emily died."

Ricki covered her mouth, her eyes widening in silent shock. Maria let out an audible gasp.

Despite her best efforts not to cry, a tear slid down Ivy's cheek. "The thing is, Jim's been acting strangely. I'm afraid he might have done something terrible—you know how much he wanted to get his hands on the person who was with Emily that night."

"No!" Ricki said in a hushed tone. "Don't say that. Jim's all talk."

The waitress arrived with their salads, momentarily interrupting them before moving off again.

Maria reached for her glass with a shaking hand. "Did you ask him if he had anything to do with Tay's death?"

Ivy gave a reluctant nod, unable to stop her lip from trembling. "He went ballistic. He grabbed me by the arms and shook me. He denied knowing anything about Tay and then he stormed out of the house. I don't know where he went. I've tried calling him, but it keeps going to voicemail. He's ignoring me. I've never seen him so angry in my life."

She wiped the tears from her cheeks and sniffed. "You remember how steamed up he was at Emily's funeral—he told a bunch of people he would kill the person who was drinking with her if he ever got his hands on them." Ivy picked at a chipped fingernail. "What if he did?"

"But he only found out this morning who the woman was," Ricki pointed out. "He couldn't have done anything to her."

"I don't know," Ivy said with a helpless shrug. "That's what he told the police. I don't know what to think. I don't know if I can trust him."

Maria let out a heavy sigh. "I wasn't going to say anything, but I'm in the same boat—unable to trust my own husband," she said, closing her eyes briefly. "Alex was lying when he said he didn't know Tay. He met up with her several times over the past few months at the lake house. Palmer told me he has a witness who saw them—I'm guessing it's Larry next door."

"What?" Ricki blinked at her in disbelief. "How did Alex explain himself?"

"He says he owed a loan shark money, and he was making payments through Tay on the debt, but he's not telling me the whole truth. I'm not sure exactly what's going on. My accountant uncovered a bunch of fraudulent invoices. I think Alex has been taking money from the company—a lot of money, enough to destroy us. And then, just this past weekend, I found some pills in his toiletry bag. He says they're antidepressants, but I don't know what to believe—he'd torn the label off. I don't know if he's an addict, or if he's dealing drugs, or what he's doing with the money." She picked at her paper napkin. "I'm afraid. What if it's Alex's fault Tay's dead?"

Ivy gaped at her. Her mind went back to the pill she'd found in Maria's hoodie. Her thoughts were spinning in a frenzied attempt to connect the dots. Could Alex have sold the drugs that killed Emily? *No!* It didn't bear thinking about. If Jim even suspected as much, he'd tear Alex apart with his bare hands. Her eyes darted between Maria and Ricki, detecting the same fear in them as she felt inside. This was rapidly devolving into an unfathomable nightmare. It wasn't just their careers that were at stake, it was their friendship too.

16

T he three women stared at their untouched salads in silence for a long moment before Ricki spoke up. "You're jumping to conclusions, Maria. I'm sure Alex had nothing to do with Tay's death. If she was mixed up in some unscrupulous loan shark business, then someone from that world may well have knocked her off. Did you ask Alex what he needed the money for?"

Maria took a sip of water. "Not yet. I wanted to finish going through all the company financials before I confronted him. He told Detective Palmer the money was to help out a cousin who'd fallen behind with his mortgage payments."

"So maybe there's a simple explanation, after all," Ricki responded.

Maria let out a snort. "I doubt it. I've never even met his cousins. They live in Australia." Her lips tightened into a thin line. "I have to go back up to the lake and talk to Larry—find out exactly what he saw. It must have been him who talked to Palmer. I'm sure Alex isn't telling the police everything. He might have been having an affair with Tay."

Ricki sucked in a sharp breath. "That's impossible—I mean, Alex would never do that to you."

Ivy chewed on her lip. "I have to agree. You've been married for twenty-six years, and you have kids together. He has too much to lose."

"I don't know," Maria said dubiously. "I think he resents how successful *XCellNourish* has become. His writing's in a bit of a slump. I didn't realize how bad things were until I snuck a look at his manuscript. He's barely written anything in weeks. Any time I ask him how things are going, he blows me off."

Ricki grimaced. "I can relate to the resentful husband part. Brock never comes right out and admits it, but the little digs and innuendos speak volumes."

"Will you come back up to the lake with me?" Maria blurted out, sounding breathless. Her eyes zigzagged with an air of desperation between Ricki and Ivy. "I don't want to confront Larry on my own. But I need to know exactly what he saw, or what he thinks he saw. If there was any kind of romantic relationship going on between Alex and Tay, I can't stay married to him—it's bad enough that he betrayed me by stealing from my company."

Ricki locked eyes with Ivy and gave a hesitant nod. "Of course, we'll come. When do you want to leave?"

"As soon as possible. Today. We can spend the night there if you don't want to drive back down the mountain in the dark."

Ricki glanced at her watch. It was almost 3:30 p.m. At this rate, they would definitely be spending the night. "Okay. I'll run home first and pack an overnight bag."

"Thank you," Maria whispered, dabbing at her eyes with her napkin. "I really appreciate your support."

"We're in this together now," Ivy added. "Jim won't return my calls, and I have no idea where he stomped off to. I could use a night away to figure out what's going on. I'm still worried he had a hand in Tay's death somehow." She reached for her purse and got to her feet. "Let's meet at my house when you're ready—I'll drive."

Ricki hurried out to her car, her thoughts racing in several different directions at once. Was this really happening? How on earth was it possible that both Jim and Alex had connections to Tay Nicholson? And why was Alex stealing money from the company? Maria had been vague about the details, but it sounded like *XCellNourish* was in danger of going under. She might not have a job after this. Everything was imploding.

She frowned when she pulled onto her street and noticed Brock's car parked in the driveway. What was he doing home? She'd given him a grocery list and asked him to make a Costco run while she was at lunch. Surely, he wasn't back already.

After tossing her car keys onto the console table, she walked into the kitchen to grab a water bottle. Her eyes widened at the sight of Brock sitting at the kitchen table, staring morosely at his phone. A bottle of vodka and a shot glass sat on the table next to him. When he glanced up at her, his eyes were bloodshot, and his hair was standing on end as though he'd been dragging his fingers through it.

"What are you doing?" Ricki asked, in a tone of confusion. "It's the middle of the day, for goodness sake." She snatched up the bottle of vodka and placed it back in the liquor cabinet before returning her attention to Brock. "Are you even listening to me?"

Before he had a chance to respond, she seized the phone from his hands and stared at the screen. Clasping a hand over her mouth, she threw him a look of alarm. "Who's this text from?"

"I don't know. I've gotten several similar messages since we got back from the lake," he said, sounding defeated.

"*Someone saw you*," Ricki read aloud. "*I know why you did it.* What's this about? Who sent you these messages?"

Brock gave a helpless shrug. "I told you I have no idea. It's a blocked number."

"What are they referring to?" Ricki asked, fully aware that an edge of steel had crept into her voice. She was shaking inwardly, fearful of the power of the emotions she'd managed to keep in check until now.

Brock got to his feet and retrieved the bottle of vodka from the cabinet. He poured himself a generous serving and chugged it back in one gulp.

"Brock!" Ricki yelled. "What is going on?"

He sank back down in his chair and buried his face in his hands.

His shoulders shook when he finally spoke. "I did something stupid —no, not stupid, something terrible."

Ricki reached for the back of her chair. "You're scaring me. Tell me this doesn't have anything to do with Tay Nicholson."

"I couldn't bring myself to say anything. It would have broken you. You were so happy, finally. Everything was going so well for you at work. I didn't want to be the one to ruin everything. But I should have told you earlier."

"Told me what?" Ricki choked out. "Is this about last weekend? I know you didn't go golfing with Dave. Where were you?"

Brock got to his feet and hobbled across to the sink like an old man. He rinsed out the vodka shot glass and turned it upside down to drain. "I can't talk about it now. I need some time to think."

"You can't just dump this on me and leave me hanging," Ricki cried.

"I'm sorry. I need to think things through first."

Ricki curled her hands into fists at her sides, seething inwardly. "If that's how it's going to be, then fine. I'm going up to the cabin tonight with Ivy and Maria. Start thinking, and when you're ready to talk, call me. I'll be back tomorrow morning. You have until then, or I'm done trying to save this marriage."

She turned on her heel and exited the kitchen feeling as if her heart was about to burst. Rage was not an emotion she was adept at handling. She was used to suppressing her anger and letting it spend itself in a more passive-aggressive manner. The intensity of what she was feeling was hugely disconcerting.

After packing an overnight bag, she left the house without saying another word to Brock, and sped across town, tormented by thoughts of what he'd done.

She managed to hold it together until she got to Ivy's house, but the minute she was inside, she slumped down on the couch and began to sob.

"Ricki! What on earth's wrong?" Ivy asked, kneeling next to her and slipping an arm around her shoulder.

Ricki lifted her head, her eyes watery with tears. "I'm sorry. I know you have enough to deal with already. I wasn't going to say anything, but I just found out that Brock's been getting strange text messages since we got back from the lake."

Ivy's brow rumpled in confusion. "What kind of messages?"

Ricki pulled a tissue from her purse and wiped her nose. "I only read a couple of them. *Someone saw you. I know why you did it.*"

She locked eyes with Ivy. "Whatever happened to Tay, I think Brock's involved too."

17

"We need to talk, Alex," Maria said, knocking on his study door and barging in without waiting for a response.

"What about?" He threw her an irritated look. "I'm trying to get some writing done. It's not easy here in town with all the distractions."

"You could have stayed up at the lake house." Maria folded her arms in front of her and pinned an icy gaze on him. "Or maybe it holds too many memories."

Alex narrowed his eyes. "What's that supposed to mean?"

"I get why you like spending time there," she went on in a willfully nonchalant tone. "It's the perfect setting for a romantic thriller, which is what you've been working on, by all accounts." She arched a brow. "Tay is such a young, sexy name for a character, don't you think?"

Alex wet his lips. "What are you insinuating?"

She tapped her fingers on her arm, eying him coldly. "Palmer tells me you did more playing then working at the lake house. That would explain the writing slump, wouldn't it, Alex? I suppose Tay was quite a distraction."

"Don't be ridiculous. She was young enough to be our daughter."

"All the more appealing to a man your age whose career is floundering." She watched her words slice through Alex like a blade, half-regretting their lethal impact. That was the thing about words—you could fling them out in half a heartbeat and spend half a lifetime trying to undo the damage they did. Still, she was only giving him what he deserved. He had betrayed her and then lied about it, made a fool of her in front of the police and their friends. "You told me you didn't know the dead woman, but you were able to give Palmer her name. He tells me a witness saw her visiting you at the lake house. What am I supposed to think?"

Alex wiped a hand over his eyes and groaned. "I swear to you I wasn't having an affair with that woman."

"Then what were you doing with *that woman*, the same woman who was found floating in the pondweed by our dock?" Maria yelled.

"Nothing!" Alex lifted his chin defiantly. "She stopped by the house once asking for directions. I didn't recognize her in the photo, at first."

Maria seethed inwardly at the blatant lie. Did he really think his secret was safe—that Palmer would cover for him like he'd begged him to?

"That's not what you told the police," Maria tossed back. "You told them you borrowed money from a loan shark Tay was working for. So either you're still lying to me, or maybe you're lying to the police too, and you really were sleeping with her, which makes you the prime suspect in her murder!"

Alex raised his hands in a placating gesture. "All right, calm down. I admit I borrowed money from her—her boss actually. He's a loan shark. At least, I think he is."

"You *think* he is?" Maria gave a disgusted shake of her head. "When are you ever going to quit beating around the bush and tell me the truth, Alex?"

"I'm trying to, if you'd listen. I ... I responded to an online ad. It was all very hush hush. I never even met Tay until the first payment was due. She insisted on collecting it in person. She came to the door and her boss, Levi, sat in the car with the engine running the entire time. I guess he comes along to make sure he gets his money. Or to rough up anyone who doesn't pay on time." He gave a helpless shrug. "I don't know much about how the underworld operates, other than the fiction I write."

Maria smirked. "And yet here you are mixed up in a real-life murder."

Alex's face paled. "We don't know for sure, yet, that it was murder. And I'm not mixed up in it. I had nothing to do with Tay's death. You have to believe me!"

"*Believe* you?" Maria sputtered. "Why should I believe anything you say? You've done nothing but lie to me. What did you need the money for anyway?"

Alex frowned and averted his eyes. "My cousin fell on hard times. He lost his job, and they were going to foreclose on his house. He has young kids and I felt sorry for him when he called me up bawling his eyes out."

Maria let out a snort. "You told me you never even met your cousins. Don't they live in Australia?"

Alex scratched the side of his neck and nodded unconvincingly. "Yes. But we're still family at the end of the day."

Maria eyed him dubiously. "Call your cousin up. Put him on speaker. I want him to confirm what you're telling me."

"It's the middle of the night over there. I can't wake—"

"I don't care what time it is! Call him up right now or I'm kicking you out of the house. I know all about the money that's missing from *XCellNourish*, Alex. Hundreds of thousands of dollars. What's really going on? What are you doing with those pills you told me were anti-depressants? Are you dealing drugs? Is that your connection to the *underworld* as you put it? Is that how you're trying to keep stride with my salary, by becoming a drug lord?"

"That's ludicrous! I told you I've been taking antidepressants."

"Only when I found the pills you were hiding from me. You tore the label off, so I have no way of knowing what they really are."

"I swear to you they're antidepressants," Alex said wearily.

Maria placed her hands on her hips. "So you expect me to believe you're depressed because you're in a writing slump?"

Alex groaned and rubbed his hands over his face. "It's not the writing."

Maria bit back the stinging retort on the tip of her tongue and took a few calming breaths to assess the situation. Alex looked truly broken. Maybe he really was telling the truth. Had she been so preoccupied with her own business that she'd failed to notice her husband was sinking into a pit of depression. Did he think she didn't care? She had loved him once. They had two incredible sons together, and a life that she adored. Up until yesterday, she'd attributed the bumps in their relationship to the normal ups and downs a marriage went through. Now, she was at a complete loss to know where they stood.

"I know you've been stealing money from the company," Maria said quietly. "I'm not sure how this is all going to shake out, but you're going to have to put it back, and quickly, or it will spell disaster for us."

Alex pulled his lips into a regretful grimace. "I can't. The money's gone."

Maria sank down on the edge of the desk and stared at him, aghast. "Gone where? Did you spend it on her? Was she blackmailing you? Did you kill her, Alex?"

"No! Stop it!" He fisted his hands, grappling with tears. "I ... I have a gambling addiction. I owed the money to Levi. The truth is, I met Tay in a casino. She was the go between—she told me she could set me up with a loan shark. That's why I lied about knowing who she was when I saw her. I knew I would be a suspect if our connection came to light, but I swear to you I had nothing to do with her death."

Maria straightened up, her penetrating gaze never leaving his face. She felt as though he was finally telling her the truth. She could read it in his eyes. He was deeply ashamed of what he'd done, but he wasn't lying anymore. Slowly, she released her breath. Her husband was an addict, but he wasn't a murderer. Her relief was momentary, her thoughts catapulting to the photo of Emily and Tay at the bar.

If Alex hadn't killed Tay, maybe Ivy was right that Jim had finally caught up with his daughter's killer.

18

Ivy squeezed Ricki's shoulder gently. "I'm sure the messages have nothing to do with Tay," she said, her tremulous tone suggesting otherwise.

Ricki pulled a tissue from her purse and mopped her tears. "Brock said he did something terrible—so terrible he couldn't even tell me what it was. You should have seen him, Ivy. He was downing vodka like it was water. That's not like him at all. He kept apologizing as though his conscience was plaguing him. It must have something to do with Tay's death. What else am I supposed to think?"

Ivy frowned. "He did seem really shaken up at the cabin. Don't you think it's odd that all of our husbands had some kind of connection to Tay? I don't know ..." Her voice trailed off as though she was considering something unpalatable. "It's almost like they were all in on what happened. They all had their reasons to do away with her—except for Brock. But he might have witnessed something."

Ricki blinked back tears. "Maybe he had the strongest reason of all. He's been spending a lot of time away from me on the weekends. He kept telling me he was going golfing with his friend, Dave, but most of the time, he wasn't with him. I checked with Dave's wife. I think he's been cheating on me."

"Oh, no! Ricki, I'm so sorry." Ivy sucked on her lower lip for a moment. "But even if he is having an affair, that doesn't mean to say it was with Tay."

Ricki sniffed and blew her nose. "You're right. Now I'm the one jumping to conclusions. It just seems like an awfully big coincidence."

The doorbell rang and Ivy got up to answer it. "That's probably Maria. Do you want to tell her about the messages?"

Ricki shrugged. "Like you said, we're all in this together."

Maria traipsed into the living room and sank down on the couch. She clasped her hands in her lap and gave a jerky shake of her head. "Before we leave for the lake, I need to bring you up to speed. I finally got Alex to talk, and it's not pretty. He admitted to a gambling addiction—a bad one. He's stolen over $600,000 from the business. But it gets worse. Tay worked for the loan shark, which means Alex is a suspect in her death, although he swears he had nothing to do with it. I don't know whether to believe him. The only thing I know for sure is that he didn't kill her himself—he doesn't have the stomach for it, even though he writes about it all day long." She rolled her eyes. "Used to, I should say. The point is, he could easily have spent some of that money he stole to hire someone to get rid of Tay."

Ivy swallowed hard. "Jim might have been in on it. If a private investigator uncovered Tay's identity, Jim would have been more than willing to help dispose of her. He still won't answer my calls or texts. I've no idea where he is." She turned to Ricki. "Do you want to tell her about Brock?"

Maria shot Ricki a curious look. "What now?"

Ricki took a sharp breath and proceeded to update her.

"The text messages mightn't necessarily have anything to do with Tay," Maria mused. "But Brock's reaction to her death was a bit odd. He seemed way more upset than any of us."

Ricki gave a sober nod. "Which is why I'm beginning to suspect he was the one who was having an affair with her.

"At this point, any one of our husbands could be involved in Tay's death," Ivy said. "And the others could be helping cover up the truth."

"We need to think this through logically," Maria said. "It's hard to imagine any of our husbands are actually capable of murder, even though they all had dubious connections to Tay. The more I think about it, the more I'm questioning Larry Thompson's involvement. I wonder how well he knew her?"

"Well enough to identify her to the police," Ricki said. "Maybe he had dealings with her too."

"He could have killed her and dumped her body by the dock in an effort to pin it on Alex," Ivy added. "He's conniving enough."

Ricki frowned. "Do you think he might have sent those text messages to Brock? His number's listed on the Prime Engineering website."

"Maybe we should talk to Larry's ex-wife—she might know something," Maria suggested.

"Do you know where she lives?" Ricki asked.

Maria nodded. "She gave me her new address before she left. I'm not sure if she still lives there, but it might be worth paying her a visit before we head up to the lake."

Twenty minutes later, they pulled up outside Sheila Thompson's modular home. "Hard to believe people accumulate this much junk," Ricki said, eying the neglected houses with distaste. "Apparently, letting the weeds grow through the trash bags alongside your house is considered ornamental landscaping in these parts."

"Not to mention scattering discarded beer cans around the front yard," Ivy added with a shudder as they climbed out of the car.

Maria rapped on a tired-looking screen door that had long since outlived its usefulness. "Sheila, are you home? It's Maria Dalcerri, your old neighbor from Tamarack Creek Lake."

The door opened and a thin woman with frizzy hair appeared. She placed her hands on her bony hips, a look of amusement in her eyes. "Well, look who the wind blew in. Miss money bags herself." She eyed Maria brazenly up and down and then turned her attention to Ricki and Ivy.

"Sheila, these are my friends, Ricki Wagner and Ivy O'Shaughnessy," Maria explained. "They were staying with me at the lake house this past weekend. You might already have heard about—"

"The body by your dock," Sheila interrupted. "Yeah, I heard. Cops came around to ask me if I knew anything about it." She folded her arms in front of her and smirked. "Partying a little too hard, were you?"

Maria stared back at her stone-faced. "Were you aware that Larry knew the dead woman?"

The smirk vanished from Sheila's face. She reached behind her for a pack of cigarettes and a lighter and then tromped down the steps letting the screen door slap closed.

"You showed me once what he did to you," Maria said, lowering her voice. "Do you think he's capable of killing someone?"

Sheila took a long drag of her cigarette. "What would his motive be?"

"Money. Would he do it for money, if someone paid him?"

A gleam of desire appeared in Sheila's eyes. She gave a casual shrug, puffing on her cigarette. "How much money are we talking about?"

"Several hundred thousand," Maria replied.

Sheila's skinny eyebrows shot up. A cold smile played on her lips as she wagged a finger in Maria's face. "It's Alex, isn't it? That's who you're talking about. You're afraid your husband hired my ex to do away with his little problem. That's what rich folks do. They never get their own hands dirty."

Maria took a step toward her. "Please, Sheila, if you know anything, you've got to help me. Has Larry offered you any money lately?"

Sheila threw back her head and laughed. "That'll be the day."

"We're going up to his place now. It would be helpful if you came with us. He might be willing to talk to you," Maria said.

"Not gonna happen." Sheila dropped her cigarette butt in the dirt and squished it beneath her flip flop. "I wish you and your girlfriends the best of luck. You're gonna need it." Without another word, she turned on her heel and disappeared inside.

"That wasn't very productive," Ivy said, as she started up the car and pulled out of the driveway. She turned to glance at Maria in the passenger seat. "When did you come up with the theory that Alex might have hired Larry to kill Tay?"

Maria flattened her lips. "It's been playing at the back of my mind ever since I caught Alex in one lie after another."

"I don't believe it," Ricki cut in. "It's too far-fetched."

"Is it though?" Maria countered. "That whole deal about Larry calling the cops on us because we were too noisy. It could have been for show—to make it look like he couldn't stand us. The police would never suspect Alex hired him to do his dirty work."

Ricki frowned. "If what you're saying is true, it's way too dangerous for us to confront Larry. You said yourself, he's threatened people before."

"I know how to handle him," Maria said. "He won't try anything with the three of us there. I need to get the truth out of him."

A little over an hour later, they pulled into the gravel driveway leading to Larry's cabin. Ivy parked out front and they picked their way through the debris in the yard to the front door. Maria pounded on it several times before Larry cracked it partway open. He eyed them suspiciously, his lips see-sawing back and forth.

"I need to talk to you, Larry," Maria said. "It's about what happened over the weekend."

"I already talked to the cops. I don't know nothin'," he growled in response. He made as if to close the door in their face, but Maria wedged her foot in the frame and waved a $100 bill in his face. "I only need a few minutes of your time."

Larry's beady eyes traveled warily over Ivy and Ricki. He grunted, then snatched the money from Maria's fist before opening the door as far as it would go. He led them into a dark kitchen and gestured for them to sit down. Ricki perched gingerly on a rickety wooden chair and surveyed her surroundings, barely able to mask her disgust. The place was even dirtier than Sheila's—it had to be rodent infested.

"You knew the girl, didn't you Larry?" Maria began, her tone soft and beguiling.

Larry let out a humph. "Not half as well as your husband did. She came knocking on my door one time asking where your place was."

"And you told her?" Ricki piped up.

Larry threw her a contemptuous look. "Stay out of this conversation. It doesn't concern you."

Ricki blinked solemnly at him. "It concerns all of us—that's why we're here. We're all under a cloud of suspicion."

"We're just trying to get to the bottom of what happened," Ivy added.

"Did you send my husband threatening texts?" Ricki asked, leaning forward on her chair.

Larry curled his lip in disgust. "I don't know what you're rambling on about." He glared at Maria. "Tell your friend either she butts out or I kick her out."

"The thing is," Maria went on, eying her nails nonchalantly, "If this turns into a homicide investigation, you'll be a suspect too, Larry. After all, you're the one with the record. I mean, the girls and I might have a speeding ticket or two between us, but that's about it." She looked around at the others and tinkled a laugh.

A deep flush crept up Larry's neck and over his ears. "I know what you're trying to do. You're not going to intimidate me."

"I'm not trying to do anything other than help you," Maria insisted, locking a corporate gaze on him. "This is your chance to negotiate. If anyone approached you and asked you to do something for them, now's the time to speak up. Before the police nail you as an accessory to murder."

Quick as a flash, Larry reached behind the door and whipped out a gun. He cocked it and moved the barrel slowly around the room. "Out! Now! Before someone else ends up a floater!"

19

Back in his office the following morning, Palmer took another look at the photo of Emily O'Shaughnessy and Tay Nicholson drinking at the bar, hoping to pick up on something significant. It was no secret that Jim O'Shaughnessy had been very vocal about what he would do if he ever got his hands on the person he believed was responsible for his daughter's death. He struck Palmer as being well capable of hunting down and eliminating the perpetrator. His theory had some merit. It was entirely possible that Tay had doctored his daughter's cocktail—she certainly had opportunity that night—but why? Had someone paid her to do it? Emily hadn't been robbed, raped, or abducted. It made no sense to suspect a crime. Yet, by all accounts, she didn't use recreational drugs. She had a steady job, a flawless record, and had graduated magna cum laude in business administration from Boston University.

Palmer leaned back in his chair and rubbed a hand over his chin. He was missing something. He needed a shot of caffeine to kickstart his sluggish brain this morning. He unfolded his lean frame from the chair and made his way down the hall to the coffee machine. The tech team member who'd unlocked Tay's phone was filling up his oversized travel mug. "Find anything useful on that device?" he asked, with a smug grin.

Palmer gave a thoughtful nod. "Yeah, there was a picture taken last year of Tay and another young woman at a bar. That woman died later the same night. Walked right out in front of a car, high as a kite. The really weird part is that her parents were staying at the lake house where Tay Nicholson's body was discovered last weekend."

The ginger-haired tech let out a long whistle as he secured the lid on his coffee mug. "Now that's an angle I wasn't expecting. I thought for sure the photo in the hidden App would be the bombshell."

Palmer tilted his head, blinking in confusion. "What hidden App?"

"I forgot to mention it when I dropped off the phone," the tech said sheepishly. "I sent you an email about it afterward. Didn't you get it? It's a free App disguised to look like a calculator. I reset the code to 1,2,3,4. There was a photo in there of a young woman and some older guy. Must have been dodgy if she buried it from prying eyes, if you know what I mean. Check it out and see what you make of it." He wiggled his brows suggestively before strolling back to his office.

Palmer snapped his mouth shut and hurriedly replaced the paper cup upside down on the stack next to the coffee maker, a sudden surge of adrenalin negating his need for a shot. Back in his office, he snatched up Tay's phone and scrolled through several screens before he came across a calculator App. It looked benign enough, not to mention the fact that it appeared to function as a regular calculator. He dutifully typed in the code the tech had given him and waited. The hairs on the back of his neck tingled when a single photo popped up on the screen. He enlarged it and studied it, his skin crawling. It was a picture of Tay Nicholson beaming at her iPhone as she snapped a selfie. Next to her stood an older man with his arm draped awkwardly over her shoulder. There was no mistaking Brock Wagner's face—his strained smile clearly indicating his fear that the photo could be used against him if it ever came to light.

Palmer shook his head in disbelief. This was becoming more

convoluted by the hour. All three couples who'd been staying at the lake house the night Tay died had some kind of connection to her— at least the men did. It stretched the bounds of credulity, but it couldn't be a coincidence. What had gone on in the house that night? A wild party? After all, they'd been drinking heavily and celebrating —the neighbor had even called the cops on them. Had Tay been high, like Emily O'Shaughnessy? Maybe she'd slipped off the dock and hit her head. He would have to wait for the autopsy results to test that theory. The timing of Tay's death certainly fit the party scenario. The medical examiner had confirmed that she'd only been in the water for a few hours. But that would mean everyone at the lake house that night had been lying to him.

Palmer scratched his jaw as he studied the photo. It was also possible that Tay's death had been no accident. If she'd threatened to tell Ricki Wagner about her affair with Brock, he might have panicked and killed her. His buddies might have helped him cover up the crime. One thing was for certain. Ricki Wagner was about to find out that her husband wasn't the man she thought he was. He had suddenly become the prime suspect in what was almost certainly a homicide.

He glanced up when Lopez walked in and set a steaming coffee on his desk.

"Last one to leave, first one to arrive, or did you crash here last night?" Lopez asked, cocking his head to one side and assessing him. "No, you shaved. You must have gone home."

"Check this out." Palmer spun Tay's phone around on the desk. Lopez bunched his brows together and scrutinized the photo. "You have got to be kidding me." He jerked his head up and stared at Palmer. "So they all knew her. She might have been an escort as well as a runner for that loan shark operation."

Palmer shoved his chair out from the desk and stood. "So far, we've got a slew of theories, an entire cast of suspects, and no answers. It's time we bring the Wagners in for questioning. We need to find out if Ricki had any idea just how cozy her husband was with

Tay Nicholson. But first, let's swing by Levi Hendrix's place again and see if he's home."

After slugging down some coffee, they left the station and drove out to Levi's address. Keeping a wary eye on their surroundings, Palmer marched up to the front door and knocked. This time they were rewarded for their efforts. A male in his early thirties, dressed entirely in black, with a shaved head and a heavily tattooed neck answered the door. The hard expression on his face made it look as if he'd have to chisel through rock to proffer a smile. He jerked his chin questioningly at them.

"Levi Hendrix?" Palmer asked, in a pleasant tone.

"Yeah?"

"May we come in?"

"Nah. I'm kind of busy right now," Levi replied, folding muscled arms in front of him.

"We're here about Tay Nicholson," Lopez said, in a somber tone. "Your fiancée?"

Levi smirked. "I don't think so. You've got your wires crossed."

Palmer kept his face expressionless. "Does she work for you, then?"

Levi shrugged. "A lot of people work for me."

Palmer made a show of pulling out his notebook. "When was the last time you saw her?"

"Couple of days ago." Levi narrowed his eyes. "Why are you asking?"

"I'm sorry to inform you that Tay Nicholson is deceased."

Levi's frown deepened, his eyes racing between Lopez and Palmer as it suddenly dawned on him where the conversation was going. "I didn't have nothing to do with it. I wasn't the only person she worked for. Anyone could have put a bullet in her."

Palmer didn't bother to correct his assumption that Tay had been shot. It was the modus mortis in the world Levi lived in. On the surface, it did seem to suggest that he'd had nothing to do with her death, but he could also be bluffing to cover his tracks.

"Where were you on Saturday night?" Palmer asked.

Levi shrugged. "Here."

"Doing what?

"Watching movies, drinking beer." Levi gave a smug smile. "Chillin'."

Palmer guessed that was probably code for shooting up. "Can anyone confirm that?"

Levi gestured with his chin over his shoulder. "My roommate."

Palmer glanced at his notebook. "I'll need to talk to him."

"Hey Digger!" Levi yelled down the hall. "Get out here. Cops wanna talk to you."

Moments later, an unwashed addict staggered down the dark hallway and blinked out at them. "Yeah, wassup?" He leaned against the wall and scratched his belly beneath a ragged Metallica T-shirt.

"I need to confirm your whereabouts on Saturday night."

Digger frowned. "I was here. With Levi."

"All night?" Palmer pressed.

Digger grinned, displaying a motley assortment of damaged teeth. "Yeah. We weren't fit to drive anywhere."

Palmer snapped his notebook shut. "One more thing. Do either of you know who Tay's fiancé is?"

Levi stuck out his jaw. "First I heard about her having a fiancé. She wasn't the type who liked to be tied down."

Palmer gave a curt nod. "We'll be in touch if we have any follow-up questions." He turned and accompanied Lopez back to the police cruiser.

"What do you make of that, boss?" Lopez asked as they climbed back in.

Palmer gritted his teeth and fired up the ignition. "If he's not the fiancé, then everything points to Brock Wagner. If he hadn't broken the news to his wife yet, it would explain why Tay wasn't wearing the ring. We need to bring him in for questioning."

"It explains the size of that rock," Lopez added drily. "By all accounts, Mrs. Wagner was making a boatload of money. If only she'd known how her husband was spending it."

Palmer's phone began to ring. He took the call, frowning across at Lopez as he listened intently to the person on the other end of the line. When he hung up, he scrubbed a hand slowly across his jaw. "The dive team found something. We just got confirmation that Tay Nicholson was murdered."

20

"I can't believe he actually pulled a gun on us," a subdued Ivy said, as she started up the engine and backed cautiously out of Larry's driveway. "That confirms what Sheila said—he's capable of violence. We should report him. He threatened us with a weapon."

"I'm not sure that's a good idea," Maria replied. "He could turn the tables on us and claim we went over there and harassed him. We were on his property, after all."

"But we weren't trespassing. He asked us in," Ricki pointed out.

Maria grimaced. "Yeah, after I stuck a $100 bill under his nose. He might tell the cops we tried to bribe him to give us some kind of alibi for Saturday night. Who knows what he's capable of dreaming up?"

Moments later, Ivy pulled into Maria's lake house driveway. The three women grabbed their overnight bags and hurried into the house, shaken by their ordeal.

Maria tossed her bag down in the hallway. "Are you sure you're okay staying here tonight?"

"We're fine. It's not as if Tay died in the house," Ivy answered.

Maria grimaced as she led them into the sunroom. "I meant, are you okay with that nutcase next door? I don't want you lying awake half the night worrying that he's going to break in and shoot us in our sleep."

Rick sucked in a sharp breath. "You don't really think he's crazy enough to do that, do you? I mean ..." Her voice trailed off. "I suppose that's the unknown, isn't it? If he killed one woman, he might not hesitate to kill again."

Ivy threw herself down in an armchair and kicked off her shoes. "Truth be told, I'm more afraid of Jim barging in here in the middle of the night and scaring us all half to death. I left him a message telling him I was going to spend the night at the cabin. He hasn't responded, yet. There's no telling what's going on in his head. He's been regressing to a dark place ever since Tay's body was discovered. All the pain of Emily's death that he never dealt with has resurfaced with a vengeance."

"He'll call you when he's ready. He probably just needs some time alone to process what happened this weekend," Maria said. She tugged off her sweater and got to her feet. "How about a glass of wine?"

Ricki gave an approving nod. "Good idea."

"Got any crackers and cheese?" Ivy asked. "I can make some snacks."

"We can do better than that. The fridge is still stocked," Maria said. "We might as well eat like queens while we're here. I have some salmon I was planning on serving that needs to be eaten."

"I'll fire up the grill," Ricki said, getting to her feet. "It won't take long to cook."

"I'll whip up a salad," Ivy added.

Ricki's phone rang and she tensed, hoping to see Brock's name. Instead, an unknown number flashed across the screen. She tossed her phone on a nearby seat and let it go to voicemail. Why hadn't Brock called her yet? Surely by now he'd had enough time to think.

After they finished their meal, they cleared away the dishes and sat around the fire pit sipping wine. "Excellent job on the salmon, Ricki," Ivy said. "Just goes to show we don't need a man to BBQ."

Maria flashed a half-hearted smile. "It's crazy to think we were all sitting around here two nights ago laughing, and joking, and relaxing. Now I don't even want to go out on my dock, because all I can think about is Tay's body floating next to it."

"I can't believe all our husbands knew her," Ivy piped up.

"And lied about it," Maria added, taking a hefty swig of wine, as if to wash away the thought. She threw a curious glance at Ricki. "Those text messages that Brock got were weird. Do you really think Larry might have been behind them?"

Ricki shrugged. "I wouldn't put it past him."

Ivy looked unconvinced. "He doesn't strike me as the techie type."

"You don't have to be techie to know how to send a text message," Ricki replied. "It's not that hard."

Maria was silent for a moment twisting the stem of her glass between her fingers. "We can't rule out the possibility that Alex might have sent those messages, if for no other reason than to deflect attention away from himself."

"So you don't believe Alex when he says he didn't kill Tay?" Ivy asked. "I mean he's an artist, a gentle soul. We all know Jim can explode in a nanosecond, but Alex has always struck me as more of a contemplative type. I can't see him lashing out in anger, and I can't picture him premeditating murder."

"To be honest, I can't imagine Jim killing anyone either," Ricki responded. "Sure, he has a temper, but he's a big softy inside. He coaches all those Little League games; it's obvious he loves kids." She stopped talking abruptly and stared down into her wine glass. "I'm sorry, I shouldn't have mentioned—"

"Please don't apologize," Ivy interrupted. "Emily's death doesn't mean we can't go on living." She rubbed a hand slowly over her knee. "I keep asking myself if Jim would be capable of killing someone who'd harmed our daughter. I don't honestly know the answer to that. Of course, he would do anything he could to defend her if someone was attacking her, but to deliberately go after someone and seek revenge—to premeditate a murder—that's different." She shook her head as if to rid herself of the thought. "If that's what he's done, I can't stay married to him."

"You're getting ahead of yourself." Maria reached for the wine bottle and refilled Ivy's glass. "We don't even know if either of our husbands were involved." She arched a brow at Ricki. "Or if Brock helped cover something up."

Ricki picked at a loose thread on the cushion she was sitting on. "He still won't tell me what he did that's so terrible. It's obvious guilt is eating him alive."

Maria looked at her earnestly. "You need to try talking to him again. If he's covering up for Alex or Jim, the best thing he can do is come clean now before he's charged as an accessory to murder."

Ricki's hand fluttered to her neck. "Brock would never make it in prison. He can't even watch a crime show without flinching. He wouldn't last a day if they locked him up." She choked back a sob and bowed her head.

Maria leaned across and squeezed her arm. "You need to convince him to talk to Detective Palmer and tell him what he knows. It has to be something to do with Tay's death. I've never seen anyone look more freaked out than he did after finding her body."

"Maria's right," Ivy chimed in. She set down her wine glass and tucked her feet beneath her. "This could all be over if you could persuade him to tell the police what he knows."

Ricki furrowed her brow. "What if it sends Jim to prison, or Alex, or both? How are you going to feel then?"

"Like we did the right thing!" Maria rejoined. "A young girl had her life snatched from her. Whoever did it should pay." She drained her glass and set it down with a thunk. "Even if all of our husbands end up behind bars, we'll survive this—I guarantee it."

Ivy stifled a yawn and staggered to her feet. "I say we make a game plan over breakfast. I'm too tired to think straight now." She gathered up their glasses and took them through to the kitchen.

"I'm just going to make sure the doors are locked," Maria said. "You guys go ahead to bed."

"See you in the morning," Ricki said, heading for the stairs.

Fifteen minutes later, she was curled up alone under the covers in the bed she'd shared with Brock just two nights earlier. Unlike Ivy and Maria, she wasn't the least bit tired. Her mind was too busy racing through everything that had happened and mulling over what might happen next.

It felt like she'd only been asleep for a few minutes when a loud banging startled her awake. She sat bolt upright in bed, fear pulsing through her veins. Maria's unhinged neighbor was the first disturbing thought that came to mind.

21

A little after 7:00 a.m. the following morning, Palmer and Lopez pulled up outside the Dalcerris' lake house.

"Let's hope Ricki Wagner hasn't done a runner," Lopez said. "You might have spooked her when you left her that message last night."

"There's a car here," Palmer said. "That's a good sign."

Lopez rang the bell a couple of times and then proceeded to bang on the door with his fist. After a few minutes, Maria answered it, a guarded expression on her face.

Palmer stepped forward. "Sorry to disturb you so early. We had a few follow-up questions for Mrs. Wagner. Her husband said she was staying here."

Maria gave a hesitant nod. "What's this about?"

Palmer rubbed a hand over his stubble. "Can we talk inside?"

Maria tightened the belt on her robe and pulled the door all the way open. "Ivy O'Shaughnessy's here too. We're all awake after that hammering on the door."

"My apologies," Lopez answered with a sheepish grin. "I tried the bell first."

"It's been acting up, loose connection," Maria said brusquely, leading them into the kitchen where Ricki and Ivy stood huddled together in hushed conversation. Their heads jerked up at the sight of Palmer and Lopez.

Ricki's eyes darted between the two officers. "What's so urgent that you had to drive all the way up to the lake? I told Brock I'd be back in Masonville Springs later today."

"It might be best if we spoke in private—"

"No!" Ricki cut him off. "You can say whatever you have to say in front of my friends. We're all in this together."

Palmer gave a wooden nod. "In that case, I need to inform you that your husband was taken into custody a couple of hours ago."

Ricki glanced uncertainly at Maria and Ivy, before returning a stricken gaze to Palmer. "I ... I don't understand."

"We're questioning him in relation to the murder of Tay Nicholson."

Ricki slumped back against the kitchen counter, her face paling. Ivy stretched out a hand to steady her.

"Brock would never ... " Ricki's voice cracked. "What evidence do you have?"

"I'll explain everything at the station. I'm going to need you to accompany me and Officer Lopez back down to Masonville Springs to answer a few questions."

"About what?" Ricki asked, sounding bewildered. "I don't know anything about Tay's murder. Are you arresting me?"

Palmer cleared his throat in an apologetic manner. "It might be best to discuss this in private."

Ricki gave an adamant shake of her head. "No. I told you already, whatever you have to say, you can say it now."

Palmer gave a grim nod. "We have some questions for you about the nature of your husband's relationship with Tay Nicholson."

"Relationship?" Ricki's voice pitched higher. "He didn't have a relationship with her."

"Are you sure about that? We found a picture of Tay and your husband on her phone—he had his arm around her."

Ricki gasped, her knees buckling. Ivy grabbed her and helped her over to a nearby chair.

"Are you certain it's him?" Ricki squeaked. Her shoulders shook as she raised a pitiful gaze to Palmer.

"I'm afraid so. We showed him the photo and he confirmed it."

"I don't believe it!" Ricki cried, half-rising out of her seat. "This has to be some kind of misunderstanding."

Ivy pulled her back down and slipped an arm around her. "It's going to be all right," she whispered, squeezing Ricki's shoulder.

"Did you have any reason to suspect your husband was having an affair?" Palmer asked.

Ricki opened and closed her mouth a couple of times. "Not really. I mean he's been gone a lot lately ... golfing."

The word came out almost as an afterthought. Palmer could tell she was beginning to connect the dots. It wasn't too much of a stretch to think that if her husband had been having a clandestine affair with Tay Nicholson, he might also have had a hand in her murder. But Palmer didn't need to spell it out for her, here and now. He'd wait until they got back to the station so he could question her in a controlled environment. He still needed to rule out the possibility that Ricki knew what her husband had done and was helping him cover it up.

"Are you ready to come down to the station and answer a few questions?" Palmer asked.

"We'll come with her," Maria cut in. She shot Ivy a quick look. "You okay with that?"

Ivy nodded, as she helped Ricki to her feet. "I'll go upstairs and give her a hand getting her things together."

"WHERE ... WHERE'S MY HUSBAND?" Ricki asked, a glazed look in her eyes. She seemed to have shriveled in on herself as she sat in the interview room clutching a plastic cup of water. She'd attempted to bring it to her lips a couple of times, but abandoned it when her hand began to shake.

Palmer clasped his fingers on the table in front of him and arranged his lips in a commiserating smile. "I just need to ask you a few questions, and then you can see him. You said your husband claimed to be golfing a lot, of late. How do you know he wasn't?"

Ricki pulled her upper lip between her teeth as if torn about how much to reveal. "I asked his friend Dave—Dave's wife, actually. She said Dave hadn't been golfing the times Brock said they'd gone together."

"So he lied to you about his whereabouts?"

Ricki gave a glum nod.

Palmer let a moment of silence unfurl to hammer home the incriminating discrepancy, before continuing.

"How would you describe your relationship with your husband?"

Ricki dropped her gaze and twisted a sodden tissue between her fingers. A sigh shuddered through her lips. "Great, up until a couple of months ago. That's when he started spending more time away from me on the weekends, some evenings as well. I thought he was jealous of my success at work. I blamed myself. I stayed late at work a lot of evenings too. He never once spent the night away from me, so I didn't suspect for a minute he was having an affair."

"Did he give any indication that he'd recognized Tay Nicholson in the photo I showed you at the cabin?" Palmer asked.

Ricki shook her head. "He was very upset about what happened, obviously. We all were." She frowned and exhaled softly as if giving herself permission to unburden herself. "But he said something strange the other day. I walked into the house and caught him knocking back shots of vodka. At first, I thought it was because he was upset about the young girl drowning. It brought back a lot of memories of Emily O'Shaughnessy's death, you see—we were very close to her. I asked him what was wrong, and he said he'd done something stupid." She choked back a sob. "First he said *stupid,* and then he corrected himself and said he'd done something terrible. But he wouldn't tell me what it was." She lifted her eyes and stared straight at Palmer. "My husband isn't capable of murder. But if Brock found the photo of Tay and Emily, and showed it to Jim O'Shaughnessy, *he* might have done something. And Brock might have helped him cover it up." She leaned across the table, her eyes glistening with a sliver of hope. "Jim swore he'd kill whoever was with his daughter the night she died."

"People say a lot of things they don't mean when they're in pain," Palmer replied.

Ricki's face crumpled. "What about Maria's neighbor, Larry Thompson? He's a monster. He carved up his ex-wife. He could have done it."

"Turns out he has an alibi. The game cameras around his property prove he didn't leave his house the night Tay's body was dumped in the lake."

Palmer shifted uncomfortably in his seat. It made no sense to prolong the agony. He bunched his brows together, arranging his face in an earnest expression. In moments like this, he always felt like a doctor about to deliver a terminal diagnosis. "Ricki, there's been a development since the body was discovered on Saturday morning."

"What kind of development?" She flicked a sideways look at Lopez who remained stone-faced and motionless, observing the interview.

"Some incriminating evidence was found. We've charged your husband in the murder of Tay Nicholson."

22

TWO MONTHS EARLIER

Tay Nicholson hunkered down behind the wheel of her beat up Saturn and watched through her oversized shades as Ricki Wagner exited the *XCellNourish* warehouse and picked her way across the parking lot, swinging a leather briefcase in one hand. Tay's gaze wandered greedily over her, probing every detail, from her confident gait to how she held herself as she strode along in her designer pumps. Her expertly coiffed and highlighted hair was not an indulgence that would fit into Tay's current budget, by any stretch of the imagination. She fingered the blonde wig that she'd purchased online. The splurge had meant subsisting on instant noodles for a week, but she considered it an investment piece. She watched enviously as Ricki waved her key fob at a luxury BMW, the kind that purred to life and smelled of leather long after it left the assembly line. Tay turned the key in the ignition of her aging Saturn, grimacing as it coughed to life. As the white BMW pulled out of the parking lot, she followed at a discreet distance, determined to learn everything she could about the woman who enjoyed the benefits of a lifestyle that would be Tay's, soon enough.

Up ahead, Ricki slowed to a crawl and signaled left before turning into the parking lot of a law office. Tay drove slowly past the building and parked on the street. She glanced in the rearview mirror to make sure she could see Ricki enter the building, and then rolled down her window to wait. To her surprise, Ricki remained seated in her car. Five minutes elapsed, before a young woman about Tay's age came bounding down the front steps of the office, a camel-colored purse flapping at her side. Her face broke into a broad grin when she spotted the BMW.

"Hey, honey!" Ricki called through the open window to her.

The young woman jogged over to the car and climbed in on the passenger side. Tay picked at the stitching on her disintegrating steering wheel cover, the taste of bile polluting her saliva. This must be Ricki's daughter—*Brock's* daughter. She hadn't known he had a child. But then she hadn't known a lot of things about him. That was about to change in a big way. There was nothing she craved more than his love, but she wasn't willing to share what he had to offer with a wife and daughter. The fiend inside her stirred, lashing its forked tongue: *something needs to be done about them.*

As she sat there simmering, her breathing came loud and ragged, as though she was underwater snatching at air through a snorkel. She gripped the steering wheel, willing herself to remain calm. This was neither the time nor the place to erupt in rage. Taking a hammer to Ricki's BMW would only appease the fiend momentarily. She had more important work to do—beginning with finding out everything she could about Brock's daughter. Information was power, and she wielded it like a maestro. After starting up her engine, she waited until the BMW was two cars ahead of her before pulling out onto the street. Fifteen minutes later, Ricki slowed to a stop outside an upscale condo. Tay tossed her blonde wig indignantly, picturing the drab apartment she currently lived in. Brock would need to do something about that, too. It wasn't acceptable that she was living below the level of luxury his daughter was accustomed to—she was entitled to more. She watched as the two women embraced, before the daughter waved Ricki off and disappeared inside the building.

Tay sat motionless in her car for a moment, debating what to do. She couldn't tail both of them. She had already amassed some useful information about Ricki, thanks to her sleuthing skills over the past few days. But the discovery that Brock and Ricki had a daughter around her age had blindsided her. He had managed to keep that from her, until now. No doubt he wanted to protect his daughter from the truth about their relationship. Tay tapped her fingernails on the dash, then abruptly turned off the engine. She would stay put, for now, and keep her focus on the daughter. With any luck, she might come back outside to check her mailbox, or go for a jog. If she reappeared, Tay would intercept her and strike up a conversation about the condos. She could pretend to be looking for something similar in the area. Her mind made up, she reached for her water bottle and took a small sip. She couldn't drink too much, or she'd have to leave to find a bathroom nearby. If the daughter didn't resurface soon, she would come back another day and try again.

Thirty minutes later, an Uber pulled up outside the condo. Right on cue, Brock's daughter appeared at the front door, dressed in designer jeans and a low-cut top, her silky natural blonde hair flowing freely over her shoulders. She jogged down to the car and hopped in, a look of anticipation on her perfectly made-up face. She must be going to meet someone—a boyfriend, perhaps.

Tay grimaced as her car sputtered to life, calling attention to its stark incompatibility with the neighborhood. The Saturn was another thing Brock would need to replace in the near future. She couldn't be expected to drive around in this piece of junk for much longer. She followed the Uber for the next twenty minutes until it dropped Brock's daughter off at an upscale bar downtown. Tay smiled to herself as she observed the woman reach for the gleaming brass handle and disappear inside. This was going to be less work than she'd anticipated. She'd learned long ago that a bar was a relatively easy way to ingratiate yourself with strangers. After parking her Saturn in a public garage nearby, Tay backtracked to the bar. Thankfully, she'd dressed up today, hoping to find an opportunity to bump into Ricki and initiate a conversation. For now, the daughter would do.

She took a quick breath before pushing open the bar's heavy

wooden front door. Inside the bustling space, she hesitated, her gaze sweeping the tables for any sign of the woman she'd been following. She frowned, her eyes combing the space a second time. She was nowhere in sight. Had she changed her mind and gone to another bar in the time it had taken Tay to park? Her exasperation built, until she suddenly spotted her coming out of the restroom. Tay bent her head and pretended to be looking inside her purse for something. She watched discreetly as the woman settled into a seat at the bar, glancing over her shoulder expectantly. Tay set her lips in a determined line. She needed to make her move before the woman's company made an appearance. The stools on either side of her were unoccupied, but she'd set her purse on the one to her right to reserve it.

"No one sitting here, I hope?" Tay asked, arching a friendly brow as she gestured to the empty stool.

The woman smiled and shook her head. "It's all yours."

Tay slid onto the leather seat, subtly inching it closer to the woman in the process.

The bartender appeared and placed his palms on the counter. His eyes darted approvingly between the two women. "What can I get you lovely ladies tonight?"

Tay let out an embarrassed laugh before glancing hesitantly at Brock's daughter. "Actually, we're not together."

The woman gave a tight smile in return.

"Two checks then," the bartender replied jovially. "What'll it be?"

After taking their orders, he swept off to mix their drinks.

"That was awkward," Tay offered with a shrug. "I'm Tay, by the way."

"Emily," the woman said, her smile softening.

The bartender deftly flipped two napkins down on the counter and set their drinks in front of them. "There you go, ladies. Enjoy!"

Tay held up her cocktail to Emily and waited for her to clink her glass. "What are we celebrating?" Tay asked with a chuckle.

"Actually, it's my birthday. I'm turning twenty-three in another hour," Emily replied. "I'm meeting a friend here and then we're going to grab dinner and go clubbing."

"What a coincidence!" Tay gushed. "It's my birthday too!"

"No way! How old are you?"

Tay peered at her over her glass with a mischievous grin. "I'll give you one guess."

Emily's jaw dropped, her glass midway to her lips. "You've got to be kidding! You're turning twenty-three too?"

Tay nodded and beamed at her. Little lies always worked best to form a connection. It was amazing how quickly people warmed up to you when they thought you had something in common, no matter how trivial.

"Are you meeting someone here, too?" Emily asked, shifting her stool around to face Tay and fixing a doe-eyed gaze on her.

Tay feigned a look of disappointment. "My boyfriend was supposed to be taking me out to dinner, but he texted to say he's running late, so I thought I'd grab a quick drink beforehand. That was over an hour ago. To be honest, he's a bit of a douche when it comes to making me wait. I've a feeling he's going to be a no show, again."

Emily let out a dramatic sigh, fluttering her impossibly long lashes. "I hear you. My boyfriend ditched me out of the blue two months ago. We were together for eighteen months, and I really thought he was the one. We graduated college together in the spring and we were talking about getting engaged and everything."

"That's horrible," Tay said, arranging her face in a faux expression of sympathy. "You must have been really cut up about it."

Emily frowned down at her glass and picked at the lime slice on the rim, her lip wobbling ever so slightly. "I was—I still am. I've been seeing a therapist."

"That's nothing to be ashamed of," Tay said softly.

Emily shrugged. "I know, but I don't want to become dependent on her."

Tay sipped her cocktail, tucking the information away. "It can't do any harm, if it gets you over the hump."

Emily's phone beeped in her purse. She pulled out a sunflower wristlet case and frowned at the screen. "Oh great! My birthday plans just went down the drain. My friend's at the hospital with her elderly neighbor. She slipped and fell in the driveway. This is turning out to be the worst birthday ever. First, my car broke down on the way to work this morning, and now this."

"I'm so sorry," Tay soothed. "That sucks—for everyone." She hesitated, and then looked at Emily with a conspiratorial smile. "My boyfriend's still a no show. How about we ditch him and go clubbing together? Celebrate our birthdays the way they deserve to be celebrated."

Emily blinked uncertainly at her. "Are you sure you want to leave your boyfriend high and dry?"

Tay rolled her eyes. "He's the one who stood me up. It'll be good for him to get a taste of his own medicine for a change. I should have broken up with him a long time ago. Maybe tonight will be the night." She raised her glass to Emily's again. This time Emily clinked it with ardor, her eyes sparkling. "To twenty-third birthdays."

Tay grinned and swallowed the last of her cocktail. *And to the lucky ones who survive them.*

23

"You know, I'm not really dressed to go clubbing," Tay said, gesturing to her black slacks and high-necked chiffon blouse. "I thought I was going to a fancy restaurant tonight. If I didn't live so far from here, I'd go home and change first."

Emily threw her a fleeting glance as she reached for her phone. "Nonsense! You look amazing," she reassured her. "I'm going to order an Uber. My dad will pick us up afterward. He doesn't like me getting a ride late at night."

Tay faked a grin to hide her disappointment. She'd secretly hoped Emily would have offered to take her back to her place and loan her something to wear. Granted, it was a long shot, but it had been worth a try. She would have enjoyed having a snoop around, maybe even getting her hands on a spare key. Not to mention the fact that it would have been a lot easier to take care of business in the privacy of Emily's condo, but it would look suspicious if Tay suggested it. That left her with only one option—endure a night of dancing and partying with Brock's nauseating daughter, while waiting for an opportunity to slip a little something into her drink. She was looking forward to watching the exemplary Emily make a fool of herself out on the town. If Brock thought his precious daughter was doing drugs, he might cut her off. If he didn't, Tay would eventually be forced to find a more drastic solution. She didn't want to have to compete for Brock's attention. Nor did she care to share him, or his money, with a daughter who was shamelessly sponging off him. There was no way *daddy's little girl* could afford to pay for that luxury condo herself, fresh out of college.

"Let's go grab something to eat first," Emily suggested, as she reached for her jacket. "There's a great pub in the old town area that serves the best fish and chips. We can have a few drinks there and decide which club we want to go to."

Nestled in a booth at the Harbor Pub and Grill, Tay made a point of letting Emily do most of the talking, gleaning as much as she could about her life in the process. She picked at the laden basket of battered halibut and fries in front of her, nodding and smiling, all the while visualizing eviscerating Brock's stomach-churning offspring. Going forward, she needed all his focus to be squarely on one woman, and that was her.

"Where do your parents work?" she asked, desperate to steer the conversation away from another long-winded story about Emily's ex.

Emily picked up a fry and dipped it in a container of sauce. "My mom works for *XCellNourish*. It's a nutritional supplement company. They're doing really well. She's been with them from the beginning, and she runs her own department now. She makes *way* more money than my dad."

Tay choked on a piece of halibut. "Sorry—that went down the wrong pipe. How does your dad feel about that?"

Emily shrugged. "He's okay with it. More power to her, I say."

"That's great," Tay said, forcing her lips into a smile. "Some men would hate to be overshadowed by their wives."

She reached for her drink and took a gulp as she fought to regain her composure. All this time she'd been lusting after the affluent lifestyle the Wagners lived, she'd assumed Brock was the one making the big bucks in his engineering firm. Not that it changed her plan, in the least. It wouldn't deter her from asking for all the things she wanted, and deserved—the new car, the upscale condo in a desirable neighborhood, the destination vacations, the expensive jewelry. In the end, she would get everything.

As Ricki's husband, Brock had equal access to her money. And with Emily disgraced—and Ricki out of the picture—Brock would be free to spend it all on her.

24

"What about your mom?" Emily asked, reaching for her drink.

"What about her?" Tay asked distractedly, still lost in thoughts of a life that would soon be within her grasp, if she kept her wits about her.

Emily laughed. "What does she do for a living?"

Tay pinched her lips together. Could she even call what her mother did *living*? She pretended to chew on her food as she concocted a suitable response. "She died of cancer when I was a teenager."

"I'm so sorry," Emily gasped. "You must miss her terribly."

"I do. She was such an inspiration. She was passionate about saving the oceans from acidification." Tay pasted a sorrowful smile on her face. "She was a marine biologist."

"Really? Maybe my dad knew her. He's a scuba diver," Emily answered, reaching for a piece of battered halibut.

Tay's mouth fell open. "A scuba diver?"

Emily laughed at her shocked expression. "Yes! Is that so hard to believe? He says he was born to dive, and my mom was born to sell. They both love what they do."

"I ... I guess I've always thought of diving as more of a hobby," Tay stammered, confusion clouding her thoughts.

"My dad's employed by a commercial dive company," Emily explained with a note of pride in her voice. "He works on underwater installation projects. It's dangerous work diving with power tools—it's not like he's swimming around all day looking at clownfish."

Tay forced a chuckle through her lips, her mind racing to piece it together. *A scuba diver.* It made no sense. Brock worked for a company called Prime Engineering. At least, that's what he'd told her—although, she'd never thought to verify it. She only ever met him in the evenings or on the weekends. She'd never seen him dressed in a business suit, or even a shirt and tie, for that matter. But why would he have lied about his job? Something wasn't adding up. Tay swallowed a lump of fish lodged in her throat. "What's your dad's name?"

Emily threw her a strange look. "Jim—Jim O'Shaughnessy. Why? Do you think your mom knew him?"

Tay's stomach dropped. It suddenly hit her that she'd got it all wrong. Emily wasn't Brock's daughter at all. What an idiot she'd been! She'd subjected herself to this sniveling piece of humanity for the past few hours unnecessarily. "I don't think she knew him. The name doesn't ring a bell." She set down her drink and got to her feet. "I need to use the restroom. Be right back."

Inside the stall, she leaned against the door and tugged her fingers angrily through her wig. How dumb could she be! In the heat of the moment, she'd let her emotions get the better of her and jumped to the conclusion that Brock had concealed the fact that he had a daughter from her. But he'd been telling her the truth all along when he'd said he and Ricki couldn't have kids. Ricki Wagner had simply been giving a coworker's daughter, whose car had broken down, a ride home. This whole mind-numbing evening had been a complete waste of time and effort. She should have stuck to her original plan and tailed Ricki instead. She might have something to show for her efforts, by now.

Furious with herself, Tay stomped out of the stall and stared at her reflection in the bathroom mirror. She needed to regroup. Maybe there was still something that could be salvaged from the night. If she could get Emily to start talking about her mom's coworker, she might learn something about Ricki that could be useful down the line. After all, the more information she had, the more power she would have over Brock.

After composing herself, she returned to the table with renewed determination to use the remainder of her time with Emily to full advantage. "How about another round of birthday cocktails?" she suggested, flagging down a passing waitress before Emily could object.

Fortified with a dirty martini, Tay pressed on with her quest to dig for information. "You seem to know this area well. Do you work downtown?"

Emily curled her lip. "I wish. I'm an intern at a law office, for now. It's not really my cup of tea, but I haven't decided, yet, what I want to do with my life. I have a business degree, but I'm not as ambitious as my mom."

Tay pounced on the opening. "I really admire your mom's drive. What's it like to run a department in a successful company?"

Emily creased her brow. "I guess she loves the thrill of it—she thrives on challenge. She's always been a take charge kind of person. It's been a crazy busy year for her. The company took off in a big way. When she first started working there, they were struggling to make payroll. Now she's in line for a stock option."

"Must be nice," Tay responded, her stomach curdling. "Does she like her coworkers?"

"Yeah, she does. Her boss is awesome, and she's pretty tight with the woman who runs the marketing department too—Ricki Wagner."

Tay pressed her fingernails into the palm of her hand to curb the tremor that ran through her at the mention of Brock's wife. It was a relief to know that he didn't have a simpering daughter, after all, but Ricki was still an issue that would have to be addressed. "Do the Wagners have kids?"

Emily shook her head as she wiped her greasy fingers on her napkin. "No. They tried for years—it's so sad. They're the nicest people and they adore me. Brock tells me all the time I'm like the daughter he never had." She smiled artlessly. "They even helped pay for my college education."

Tay recoiled as though she'd been lanced through the heart. A sudden surge of jealous rage flash-flooded through her veins as she fought to keep her emotions locked behind an amiable expression. "They sound like very sweet people."

Emily nodded and flashed her annoyingly perfect teeth. "Where do you work?"

"At Home Depot—accounts payable," Tay lied smoothly. "Boring as the day is long."

Emily giggled. "I bet. All those rednecks. Hey, I've got an idea. How about we make a pact to hand in our resignations and find more interesting jobs before our next birthday?"

"I'll drink to that," Tay said, raising her glass. She swallowed a sip of her martini, relishing the hint of olive as the liquid slid down her throat. She was still reeling from Emily's revelation and contemplating what to do about it. It seemed as if Brock's and Ricki's inability to have children of their own had only intensified their affection for Emily Goody Two Shoes O'Shaughnessy. If they'd helped pay for her college education, who knew what else they had done for her. There was even a possibility they might have written her into their will. Tay grimaced at the disturbing thought. That wouldn't do.

That wouldn't do at all.

25

At the Escapade Club later that evening, Tay plied Emily with drinks at every opportunity. As the night wore on, her plan began to take shape. She would slip some fentanyl into Emily's drink when they were almost ready to leave, and then send a text from Emily's phone asking Brock to pick her up—explaining that she was wasted and didn't want her dad to find out. Brock wouldn't be so enamored with his surrogate daughter if she ended the night high as a kite. It would be the beginning of the end of their oh-so-perfect relationship. Tay had already figured out Emily's password—she'd observed her typing it into her phone on multiple occasions over the course of the evening. She'd also taken the opportunity to rummage through Emily's purse while she was flirting with some loser on the dance floor and had slipped a few pills into her zippered makeup pouch. It would confuse Emily when she discovered them later and make it harder for her to talk her way out of the situation. Even if she managed to convince Brock that she hadn't voluntarily ingested fentanyl, it would be impossible to say for sure who had spiked her drink. They had danced with several different guys and shared cocktails with a couple of them at their table. Any one of them had ample opportunity, and, presumably, motive.

Tay was sorely tempted to spike Emily's drink with enough fentanyl to make her overdose, but that was a step too far. If Emily had been Brock's daughter, Tay wouldn't have hesitated. But all she really needed to do now was make sure that Emily disgraced herself so that Brock stopped viewing her through rose-colored glasses. The thought of him bestowing any affection on Emily O'Shaughnessy—biological daughter or not—repulsed her. She wanted his undivided love and attention. She would finish what she'd started here tonight, and then she would deal with Ricki.

"I'm done! My legs are about to give out!" Emily exclaimed, as she sank back down in the booth next to Tay.

"He was pretty cute," Tay said, gesturing with a tilt of her chin to the dark-haired guy Emily had been dancing with.

"Sadly, he has a girlfriend. She's working tonight," Emily answered, sounding disgruntled. "Good-looking and faithful, why can't I find a guy like that?"

"They're hard to come by," Tay agreed. "But hey, the night's not over. Here comes the man of your dreams right now."

Emily ran an appraising eye over the handsome stranger approaching their table. "Okay, I'm in," she muttered to Tay, before scrambling back to her feet.

Clutching a beer in one hand, the tall blue-eyed man with a sun-streaked ponytail grinned as he pulled Emily onto the dance floor.

Tay watched them merge with the pulsating mass of bodies before checking the time on her phone. It was after midnight—time for Cinderella to leave the ball. With a deft flick of her wrist, she dropped two pills into Emily's drink and then reached for her own glass and casually took a sip. She set down her drink and dipped her hand into Emily's purse, fishing around for her phone. She smirked as she sent Brock a pitiful plea for a ride home. If only he knew who was texting him. Of course, she would slip away into the shadows when he showed up—he could never know she'd been here tonight.

While she waited for Emily to return, she turned down a couple of inebriated dance partners buzzing around her table with the desperate air of flies about to expire. She had paced herself over the course of the evening, even disposing of a couple of drinks when Emily wasn't paying attention, needing to remain clear-headed. Her thoughts drifted to the luxury condo where Emily lived, and her stomach knotted. It wasn't right that she had successful parents of her own as well as surrogate parents who idolized her. For a minute or two, Tay toyed again with the idea of throwing a few extra pills into Emily's drink, but she nixed the notion. The last thing she needed was for her nemesis to overdose here in the club. The place would be swarming with cops within minutes and making a discreet exit would prove tricky. Restraint and discretion would get her what she wanted in the end.

A short time later, Emily reappeared with ponytail guy in tow. Tay gritted her teeth, trying to mask her exasperation. She couldn't have a stranger hanging around watching Emily slur her words and stagger out of the club—he might ask too many questions. She would have to scare him off somehow. Emily flopped down on the seat next to her and reached for her glass. She took a long swig of the doctored drink and let out a satisfied sigh. "Ugh, I was parched. I'm done dancing for the night." She flapped a hand at the guy next to her. "Tay, this is Nate. Nate, this is Tay. We share the same birthday, and we're the same age, can you believe it? How about you two get to know each other while I visit the ladies room?" Without waiting for a response, she lurched to her feet and teetered off into the shadows at the back of the club.

Tay placed her elbows on the table and interlaced her hands. "Nice meeting you, Nate. Now, clear off. Emily lives with her boyfriend and he's a police officer." She glanced dramatically at her watch. "His shift ended at midnight. He should be showing up any minute now to drive us home."

Nate pulled his sun-bleached brows together and tightened his grip on his beer bottle. "Yeah, see you around. No hard feelings." Tay watched him slink off, her lips curling into a satisfied grin. Minutes later, she spotted him on the dance floor, one arm curled around the waist of a redhead in a skintight dress who was swaying provocatively in front of him. The minute Emily returned, Tay wasted no time pointing Nate out to her. "You had a lucky escape with that one. He didn't hang around for two seconds after you left."

"You've got to be kidding me! Why do I only ever attract losers?" Emily wailed, clutching the edge of the table as she sank back down in her seat. "I ... I feel woozy all of a sudden."

"I'm ready to call it a night. We've both had one too many cocktails," Tay replied, swiftly gathering up her things.

Emily reached for her purse and stood, swaying on her feet. Tay linked an arm firmly through hers and began maneuvering her over to the exit door. "You really are in bad shape, aren't you? Want me to call your dad to pick you up?"

Emily shot her an alarmed look. "No! I can't let him see me like this. I'll order a ride." She staggered outside the club and over to a small retaining wall and slumped down on it. She dug her phone out of her purse and fumbled with it for several minutes, muttering in frustration when it slipped from her fingers.

Tay knelt down and retrieved it from the curb. "You got lucky," she said in a reproving tone. "The screen's not cracked. Sure you don't want me to text your parents?"

"I said ... no!" Emily shrieked, snatching the phone from her hand.

Several bystanders cast amused looks her way, clearly enjoying the spectacle.

"How about I text Brock then?" Tay suggested casually. "I bet he'd come get you."

Emily narrowed her eyes at her. "Why don't you just get lost?" She yanked her purse over her shoulder, wobbling as she got to her feet.

"Fine! I tried!" Tay raised her palms placatingly in front of her. "I'll leave you to it."

A couple of bystanders smirked at her, and she shrugged in response. She pulled out her phone and set about ordering an Uber, secretly pleased at the scene Emily had caused. She would have got even more satisfaction if she could have waited around to see the expression on Brock's face when he arrived and saw the state Emily was in, but this was the next best thing. She scrolled through her ride options, her finger poised to confirm her choice when the squeal of tires distracted her. A woman's piercing scream cut through the night, abruptly ending the laughter and chatter.

Tay jerked her head up in time to see Emily land in a crumpled heap in the middle of the road.

26

Tay curled her fingers around her coffee mug, as she reflected back on the night Emily had died. It was hard to believe she'd been gone almost two weeks already. The evening had taken a final jaw-dropping twist Tay hadn't anticipated, but it had been most rewarding. Fate had intervened on her behalf, and who could argue with that? Granted, she'd had a hand in Emily's death, but as it turned out, it wasn't the drugs that killed her. Emily had stupidly stepped out into the middle of the road and tried to flag down an Uber. She hadn't even noticed the speeding Suburban coming from the other direction that had slammed into her. It was all over in one sickening crunch. One sloppy misstep. As the horrified onlookers swarmed around Emily's body, and pandemonium took hold, Tay had quietly slipped away. Tempting as it had been to wait around and see Brock's reaction, she had wisely refrained.

She hadn't known for sure that Emily had died until the morning after the accident, when the local news confirmed that a pedestrian had been struck by a car and succumbed to her injuries outside the Escapade Nightclub.

"Witnesses tell us the deceased appeared to be intoxicated when she stepped out into oncoming traffic. Police are interested in talking with a young blonde woman who was seen in the club with the victim earlier in the evening," the newscaster read in a monotone before moving on to a story about a local politician facing corruption charges.

The bartender at the club had given the police a description of Tay, but it was worthless information. Tay chuckled as she lifted her coffee mug to her lips, remembering how he'd remarked on her beautiful blue eyes at one point in the evening. The colored contacts had been well worth the paltry price she'd forked over for them on Amazon, and the blonde wig had already paid for itself several times over.

Her phone pinged with an incoming text, and she set down her mug to read the message. She furrowed her brow in irritation. She wouldn't allow Brock to cancel his plans with her for a second weekend in a row. She hadn't anticipated how deeply Emily's death would affect him—maybe it was because he'd come on the scene minutes after it happened. A photographer had snapped a photo of him kneeling in the street by her bloodied body, his face contorted with grief. He'd been as destroyed as if he'd been her own father— even breaking down on the phone with Tay when he described the funeral a few days later. "It's so wrong," he choked out. "No one that young should die. She was just starting out in life. Emily was such a beautiful girl, inside and out. Her parents are shattered."

"I imagine they must be devastated," Tay responded primly.

"Jim's beside himself, poor guy," Brock went on, seemingly oblivious to her taut tone. "The medical examiner said she had drugs in her system, but Emily didn't do drugs. Jim's convinced someone spiked her drink at the club. If he's right, they'd better hope the police get to them before Jim does."

Tay fought to keep the exasperation out of her voice. "Didn't you say it was her birthday that night, and her plans fell through? Maybe she decided to let loose with a pill or two after her friend stood her up. One of the guys at the club might have offered her a little birthday cheer." She laughed. "No harm in that. She was a grown woman."

Brock had practically jumped down her throat. "It's not funny, Tay.

I thought you of all people would be more sympathetic. Have a little respect."

They'd ended up having their first argument about it—a gnarly one at that. Brock had called her back the following day and apologized, somewhat stiffly, Tay noted. He'd proceeded to tell her ad nauseam about how he and Ricki were putting together a photo album of memories of Emily for Jim and Ivy. Tay seethed inwardly as she pictured Brock and Ricki, heads huddled together over their emotionally bonding craft project. From what Tay had observed, Emily's death had only served to bring Brock and Ricki closer together. Another hitch in her plan she hadn't foreseen. Ricki was a problem she would have to deal with sooner rather than later. The last thing she needed was for the Wagners to attempt to revive bygone days of wedded bliss.

Eliminating Ricki would be a little like killing the golden goose, but Tay had found out that she had a hefty life insurance policy which would pay out in the case of accidental death—something that would require meticulous planning. She wasn't overly concerned about the details. She was up for the challenge. It was simply another bridge that had to be crossed.

In the meantime, she could have a little fun running interference with Ricki's perfect life. She would begin by finding a way to sabotage her *XCellNourish* stock option.

27

Tay spent the next few days researching everything she could find about *XCellNourish* and its founder. Envy moved through her like a toxic vapor when she learned how successful the company had become in a relatively short space of time. No wonder Ricki was driving around in a late model BMW. It was sickening to read about Ricki's lavish praise of her boss's trailblazing vision and dynamic leadership. Maria Dalcerri sounded like an egotistical autocrat. Tay would enjoy taking her down a peg or two, while she finalized her plans to destroy Ricki.

After observing Maria and Alex Dalcerri for several days, and studying their online profiles, Tay determined that Alex was the weaker target. He struck her as more of a tortured artist than a roaring success in his field. Not to mention the fact that he was a man, and Tay was confident in her powers of seduction. She'd also gleaned an interesting tidbit about Alex Dalcerri that made him the perfect entry point for her plan. He liked to gamble. Even more intriguing was the discovery that he gambled during the day when Maria was at work, which led Tay to believe that Maria was unaware that her husband was busy squandering the money she was making, instead of working on his writing career. If Tay's hunch was right, and

Alex was an addict, she knew exactly how to work the situation to her advantage—she specialized in addiction.

Later that week, seated at a craps table in the *Lone Diamond Casino*, dressed in a low-cut top and skinny leather pants, Tay fluttered her false eyelashes in Alex's direction as he leaned over the table to roll the dice, allowing him a generous view of her cleavage. It didn't escape her notice that his eyeballs remained firmly fixed on the dice. Sweat beaded on his forehead as he gripped the edge of the table with an air of sunken desperation. Tay smiled inwardly. If she couldn't seduce him with her assets, she knew she could seduce him with the lure of additional cash to fund his habit. It wouldn't be the first time she'd introduced some unwitting soul to Levi Hendrick—a loan shark who swallowed his victims whole like an unsuspecting vertebrate. He gave her a cut of the profits in return for her services. Unscrupulous, and ruthless when it came to collection, Levi didn't just deal in laundered money. He could supply almost anything, like the fentanyl Tay had put in Emily's cocktail. She was even considering asking him to help her with the Ricki situation, but she'd have to tread carefully. If the hit was not perfectly executed, and the police suspected foul play, it was never good to have people who could talk in return for immunity.

After playing several rounds of craps, and blowing all the money she'd wheedled out of Brock last week, Tay hung around the tables until Alex had run through all his chips. She followed him across the casino floor and sidled up to him when he stopped by a roulette wheel, a crazed look of guilty anticipation on his face.

"Hey there! I saw you at the craps table earlier. How'd you fare?" Tay asked.

Alex threw her a distracted look. "Uh, not good. Not good at all, actually." He folded his arms in front of him and frowned at the roulette wheel. "I think I just need to change games. I wasn't on a winning craps streak tonight."

"It was a cold table," Tay assured him. "I blew three hundred bucks on it."

Alex's head jerked around with an air of camaraderie. His eyes traveled over her, lingering on the diamond studs that Brock had reluctantly bought her after she'd insisted on dragging him into the most expensive jewelry store in town. Alex's brow rumpled, wondering, perhaps, why she hadn't pawned the diamonds.

Gathering herself, Tay hitched her lips up into a convincing smile. "I don't normally bother with craps. I'm a poker player. That's where I make my money." She knew this would catch his interest. Any time she'd observed him in the casino over the past couple of days, he'd been a fixture at the poker tables—only occasionally wandering over to a craps table or a roulette wheel to take his chances on making up what he'd lost.

"Really?" Alex said. "I've never seen you at the tables before."

"I just moved here from Las Vegas," Tay replied. "My mom has terminal cancer."

Alex scratched the back of his neck, his eyes following the tiny white ball circling the roulette wheel as it slowed. "Sorry to hear that."

Tay gave a small shrug of acknowledgment. "Thankfully, the money I make from playing poker allows me to hire excellent care for her. She wants for nothing."

Alex turned to her, a gleam of interest in his eyes. "How does someone as young as you make a living from playing poker? I thought only the best players were able to live off their winnings."

Tay gestured toward the bar at the edge of the casino. "Buy me a drink and I'll spill some of my secrets."

A couple of cocktails later, and Alex was eating up everything Tay was telling him.

"Poker's more a game of skill than luck. Never react to your cards out of fear," she said, wagging a finger playfully at him. "Take control. The first step is to find a table with bad players. That's where you can make some serious money. The other important thing is that you need to go big or go home."

Alex stared glumly into his glass. "I'm walking on the edge as it is. I can't risk too much right now. All of our money's tied up in my wife's company. She's killing it. I'm an author, but I haven't published anything in a while."

None of this was news to Tay. She swished her counterfeit locks over one shoulder and peered across at him from beneath her false eyelashes. "Let me guess, your wife doesn't know how much you've gambled away."

Alex's shoulders sagged. "Not yet. But she's going to find out, sooner or later."

"What if you could win it all back in one fell swoop?" Tay asked smoothly. She lowered her voice. "I know a guy who can set you up with a line of credit—enough to make it happen. No questions asked. I used him when I first got started."

Alex frowned, his eyes glittering at the prospect of a fresh influx of cash. Clearly, he was torn—weighing the chance of digging an even deeper hole against the possibility of freeing himself from the no-win situation he was in.

Tay sipped her drink nonchalantly, careful not to press him or rush his thought process. He didn't strike her as particularly bright—insipid was the word she'd use to describe him. For the life of her, she couldn't understand what Maria saw in him. Other than the fact that he was an attractive-looking man for his age, there was nothing about a washed-up writer who had long since sold his soul to poker chips that was appealing. He and Maria had probably met while they were still in school—evidently, she had far outstripped his career since then. No doubt, that was a large part of the reason he was whiling away his days in casinos. He probably couldn't deal with the feelings of inadequacy as his wife's business exploded, while his career tanked. Tay set down her cocktail glass and gave him her full attention. Time to stroke his ego before she went in for the kill. "What kind of things do you write?"

"Fiction. I've only published one book so far," Alex answered. "I'm working on another but it's slow going."

"What's it about?" Tay asked.

"It's an international espionage thriller."

Tay gaped at him. "No way! That's my absolute favorite genre. I'm super impressed that you've written a book. I bet your wife's blown away by that."

Alex sat up a little straighter and puffed out his chest. "She'd be more impressed if I finished the one I'm working on right now. She doesn't understand the artist muse. I can't turn it on and off like regular business hours. She's all about productivity and efficiency. That doesn't apply in my line of work."

"Of course not," Tay agreed. "You need time and space to allow the ideas to percolate."

"That's what I've been telling her, but she keeps hounding me to get a system going—pages per day, or some such thing. I can't work that way. It makes it harder to get the creative juices flowing. She doesn't get it. She's got every last minute of her day scheduled."

Tay tightened her lips and gave a reproving shake of her head. "It's her fault you're in this mess. She's driving you to it by stressing you out."

Alex frowned. "I don't know if I'd go that far. I made the choices I made."

Tay laid a hand on his arm, making sure the large diamond on her left hand was on full display. "So make the choice to get out of it. *Believe*. Like I said, you gotta think big."

She reached for the Coach purse Brock had bought to appease her after their argument, making a point of setting it directly in front of Alex as she rummaged around for her phone.

"Give me your number and I'll text you mine," she said. "Just in case you change your mind about that loan."

"Uh, okay," Alex mumbled.

Tay typed the number he recited into her phone and then slipped it back into her purse, noting with satisfaction that Alex was eying the Coach logo with a contemplative air as she got to her feet. With a carefree wave, she turned and walked out of the casino, grinning to herself.

He would call her—she was certain of it. And once he was hooked, *XCellNourish* would begin leaking cash at a rate a third-rate poker player like Alex could never hope to repay.

28

It was almost a week later before Alex reached out to her, but when he did, it was evident he was desperate for a fix. Tay quickly made the necessary introductions over a secure phone line and then acted as go between, ferrying the loan installments in bundles of cash from Levi to Alex, and encouraging him to take out increasingly larger amounts. He was a fixture at the poker table every day after that. Within a relatively short space of time, he'd run up a tab of several hundred thousand dollars. At two-hundred percent interest, paying it back would be no small feat. When Levi informed him that he was unwilling to front him any more money, Alex had been panic-stricken. "I just need a little more time. I know I can make it back."

"Can't you just ask your wife for the money?" Tay had asked, blinking innocently at him.

"It's not that simple," Alex ranted, dragging his hands through his hair. "She'll kill me if she finds out what I've done."

Tay shrugged. "Then, don't ask. Just take it."

Alex had stared at her, jaw askew, but she knew his gears were whirring, and she'd planted a seed.

Tay snickered to herself as she recalled the sheen of sweat that had formed on his forehead as he wrestled with her suggestion. She almost felt sorry for him. After all, he wasn't her real target—he was merely collateral damage. And knocking Maria off her pedestal was simply a diversion. Destroying Ricki was still her main objective. With interest charges racking up, and Levi tightening the noose, she was betting Alex would have little choice but to siphon money from *XCellNourish* to settle his debts. It might not prove to be enough to topple the company, but it would surely knock the stock option Ricki had been promised off the table. Tay was sick and tired of listening to Brock bragging about it—bragging about Ricki, period. Thankfully, she wouldn't have to endure it for too much longer. She was putting the final touches on her plan to deal with Ricki once and for all.

Her phone began to ring, and she dug it out of the side of the couch and turned down the volume on the television to take the call. "Hey, Alex! About time I heard from you. Levi's patience is wearing thin. Are you at the casino?"

"Yeah, I just stepped outside for a minute. Listen, I need you to tell Levi I've come up with the full amount. I want to pay my loan off ASAP."

Tay's eyebrows shot up in surprise. She straightened up on the couch and pressed the phone to her ear. "Wow! That's great. How'd you get the money together so quickly?"

Alex cleared his throat. "I hit the jackpot on the slots."

Tay burst out laughing. "Sure you did."

"Why's that so hard to believe?" Alex grumbled.

"For starters, I've never even seen you play the slots before."

"You don't know everything about me."

A smug grin crept across Tay's face. She knew a lot more that he realized. "Look, it's none of my business how you got the money together. I'm just the runner. Want me to set up a time with Levi? It's got to be cash."

"Can't I just give it to you?"

"It doesn't work that way. You know Levi likes to be there to collect the payments and make sure there's no funny business."

"Fine, but we can't meet here in town. Come to the lake house."

"When?"

"This weekend. I'll have the place to myself. How's this going to work? Will he come in and count the cash for the payoff?"

"No. I'll handle it. Levi will wait in the car, as usual. He doesn't ever let his clients see his face." She hesitated for a moment before adding, "Not unless it's the last face they see."

"Are you serious?" Alex hissed into the phone. "You never said he was dangerous."

"He's not, unless he has to be," Tay answered in a lighthearted tone. "By the sound of it, you have everything under control, so you have nothing to worry about, do you?"

"He's not going to bring a gun, is he?" Alex asked, sounding subdued. "I don't want any trouble."

"There won't be any trouble," Tay purred. "Just keep up your end of the bargain and we'll all part on good terms."

There was a beat of silence before Alex said, "You don't really make your money playing poker, do you? You make it luring suckers into your loan shark scheme. I suppose you get a cut or something."

Tay rolled her eyes. It had taken him long enough to figure it out. "It's not a scheme, Alex. It's a business. A woman's got to make a living somehow."

She hung up, smirking as she tossed her phone onto the couch and snuggled beneath her fuzzy blanket. Alex had come up with a lump sum to pay off his debts, after all. Of course, he was lying about winning big at the casino. And he couldn't have asked his wife for the money—he'd already made it clear she'd kill him if she knew what he'd done. Tay had a good feeling about this. If Alex had stolen the money from *XCellNourish* to settle his debts, the ripple effects would be catastrophic. Ricki's life of luxury was about to come tumbling down.

29

Ricki swerved her BMW back into her lane at the very last minute, narrowly missing a Ford F-150 truck, whose furious occupant raised a fist to her in passing. She wasn't usually a distracted driver, but this morning she was racing to drop off her dry cleaning on her way into the office for an important meeting with a potential new distributor. The close encounter with the truck spooked her, and she slowed her speed, breathing out a sigh of relief when she spotted an open parking spot directly in front of the dry cleaners. Precious minutes saved right there. She couldn't afford to be late for work this morning. Maria was in New York on a business trip and depending on her to close this deal.

After turning off the ignition, she reached into the back seat for her silk blouses and Brock's jacket. He hadn't asked her to take it to be cleaned, but she'd noticed a small stain on it when she was organizing her closet over the weekend. She did a quick check of the pockets and tossed a receipt into the console before heading into the dry cleaners. Moments later, she returned to her car and climbed in.

Spotting the crumpled receipt, she unfurled it and glanced distractedly at it, preparing to toss it in the trash. Her eyes widened in disbelief at the staggering total. $11,315. Her gaze traveled slowly up the slip to the business name at the top—*Harlowe's Fine Jewelry*. What on earth had Brock purchased at a jewelry store for that amount? They never spent that kind of money on each other—not even now that she was making three times the salary she'd started out at. She studied the line item next to the total: 1.5 CT certified solitaire. Was that a ring?

For several minutes she sat staring at the receipt trying to figure out what exactly she was looking at, before she remembered her meeting. Slipping the receipt into her purse, she started up the engine, a feeling of disquiet building inside her. The receipt was dated over a week ago and Brock hadn't dropped any hints that he'd bought her anything special. Only a few days earlier, they'd celebrated their 22nd wedding anniversary. She'd given him a vintage copper fishing lure and he'd given her a copper sign with their name and house number—something she'd been wanting for a while. Modest but thoughtful gifts that were more their style.

By the time she reached the office, her gut was awash with doubt and uncertainty. She wasn't sure she'd be able to attend the meeting, let alone give a convincing presentation. She hated to leave Ivy in the lurch to handle things, but it would be better than botching the pitch to a potential new business partner. She couldn't afford to let *XCell-Nourish* down. The company had given her everything—it wasn't the money as much as the purpose it gave her. It had been hard accepting the fact that her body would never be able to carry a child. In years past, she and Brock had discussed adopting but decided against it, in the end. They had settled for a puppy, and promised each other they would travel extensively, which had never transpired. Over the past few years, *XCellNourish* had consumed her every waking thought as she'd worked tirelessly alongside Maria and Ivy to make it a success.

In the corporate bathroom, she splashed cold water on her face and pinched her cheeks to bring a little color to them, hoping she could hold things together long enough to get through the meeting. She frowned at her reflection in the mirror as she pulled out her lipstick. Beneath her immaculate makeup she was an emotional wreck. Why had Brock purchased a diamond? Was there another woman in his life, occupying his attention? She couldn't even remember the last time she and Brock had spent a day just hanging out together. Was it possible he was filling his time with someone else?

She hadn't seen the jewelry store charge on their joint credit card which meant he must have put it on his personal card. Was he hiding other charges from her too—hotel rooms, flowers, dinners she hadn't been present at? Acid frothed in her throat. She needed to get into his phone and retrieve his login information for his credit card so she could check the statement online. She would confront him once she knew the full extent of what she was dealing with.

The day seemed to drag on indefinitely. Somehow, she stumbled through her presentation on autopilot. Despite her best attempt to drum up an air of confident optimism, her pitch had been somewhat lackluster, and the client hadn't indicated if he was going to sign on with them or not. It was a disheartening outcome. She'd been hoping to call Maria later that day with the good news that they'd secured the deal. It would have been the perfect feather in her cap before their weekend trip to the lake tomorrow to celebrate their best quarter ever. Instead, she'd likely jeopardized a lucrative distribution channel that might end up going to a competitor.

After the meeting, Ivy had asked her if she was feeling all right. Ricki had lied and said she thought she was coming down with something. Ivy encouraged her to leave early, but Ricki didn't want to spend hours pacing around the house waiting on Brock to return. She whiled away the rest of the afternoon holed up in her office, staring into space for the most part, questioning all the golf Brock had been playing of late. She'd been happy for him when he'd found a hobby he enjoyed, but was there more to it? Had he met someone at the golf club? On impulse, she picked up the phone and called Dave's wife. "Hey Kate, how are things with you?"

"Oh, you know. Busy ferrying kids between soccer practice and orthodontic appointments. Nothing glamorous in my daily routine." She gave a good-natured chuckle. "How's everything on your end? Dave tells me business is booming."

"It is. We just had our biggest quarter ever."

"Good for you! You deserve the success after all those long hours you put in to get that start-up off the ground," Kate replied.

"Thanks." Ricki let out a dramatic sigh. "I don't think Brock's too excited about me working weekends. I'm glad he's got golf to distract him. Speaking of which, did he happen to leave his gloves in Dave's car last Saturday?"

"Last Saturday," Kate echoed in a questioning tone. "No. Dave didn't play golf last weekend. We were out of town for my aunt's sixtieth. Poor Dave. Between soccer games and family obligations, he hasn't had a chance to swing a club in weeks."

Ricki squeezed the smiley face stress ball on her desk tightly in her fist, distorting its grin into a flinty line of disapproval. "Gotcha. Brock probably left his gloves at the club. I'll call and see if anyone turned them in."

She hung up and slumped back in her seat, blood pounding in her temples. If Brock hadn't gone golfing with Dave in weeks, who was he going golfing with? The jewelry receipt had suddenly taken on an ominous significance.

On her way home from the office later that evening, she picked up Chinese, too tired to come up with anything more creative than chicken curry and fried rice. She'd long since given up any attempt to cook dinner. More often than not, both she and Brock were working late. When she heard his car pull into the driveway forty-five minutes after she arrived home, her stomach muscles clenched. She wanted to arm herself with more information before she confronted him. She would have to act normal and pretend there was nothing wrong until he went to bed, and she could sneak a look at his phone.

"You beat me to it," Brock said, tossing his briefcase onto a chair. "First time this month."

"Didn't know we were keeping track," Ricki shot back, cringing at her icy tone. The last thing she wanted to do was arouse Brock's suspicions before she'd done a little digging.

He raised his brows. "Rough day at the office?"

Ricki sighed. "I botched my presentation, and the distributor didn't sign the contract. He says he needs some time to think it over. Maria's going to be disappointed when she gets back from New York this evening. She did all the groundwork. All I had to do was close the deal."

"Don't be so hard on yourself. I'm sure you did great," Brock responded, pulling her toward him and kissing her on the forehead before she could sidestep his embrace. "I bet the distributor will call tomorrow, eager to jump in with both feet after he's had a chance to look over the contract."

"Let's hope you're right or my job could be on the line." Ricki gestured to the food. "I picked up dinner if you're hungry."

"Thanks. I already ate a sandwich earlier. I'm going to shower and turn in. I have to be up early for a meeting at our branch office over on the east side tomorrow. It'll take me at least an hour to get there in rush hour traffic."

Ricki watched his retreating figure as he climbed the stairs. She reached for the TV remote and clicked on a documentary about fast food, muting the sound so she could hear the shower turning off. She waited almost twenty minutes before tiptoeing up the stairs and peering into the bedroom. Brock was out cold, snoring softly. She crept over to his side of the bed and quietly unplugged his phone, before retreating back downstairs. Nestled among the pillows on the couch, she typed in the date they met—a password they both shared —and then clicked on his Gmail App. She'd never snooped on his phone before, but then she'd never had any reason to. For several minutes, she perused his emails, but nothing struck her as anything bordering on betrayal. Switching direction, she opened up his messages, and tapped on a number that was listed simply as *D* in his contacts.

Why are you holding out on me? It makes me think you don't love me.

A knife twisted in Ricki's chest as Brock's response swam before her tear-filled eyes.

Of course I love you. Can you meet tomorrow? We can talk then.

30

Ricki lay curled up in a tight ball on the couch, clutching a crumpled tissue in her fist as she fought back tears. How could she have been so stupid? How could she not have realized what was going on? Brock had never shown more than a passing interest in golf in all the years they'd been married. It was completely out of character for him to suddenly become obsessed with the game. If he hadn't been playing golf with Dave for the past few weeks, he'd probably been lying in other instances too—like when he said he was going to the driving range or taking a lesson. In fact, it was entirely possible he'd never played golf at all. She'd seen him loading the clubs he'd purchased into the car on multiple occasions, but that was as far as it went. He could have been going anywhere. She'd never questioned him—never had any reason to check the clubs to see if they'd been used. She'd been so consumed with her work that she hadn't paid any attention to his extra-curricular activities for some time now. Truth be told, they were living parallel lives. She was fulfilled by her job, and she'd taken it for granted that Brock was happy too. Apparently, he was—just not with her.

It was past midnight before Ricki finally dragged herself to her feet and padded quietly up the stairs. She plugged Brock's phone back into the outlet and stood staring silently at the tousled head of the man who had seen her at her worst—held her and cried with her over their infertility. She loved him, yet, in this moment, she hated him too. Rage ebbed and flowed inside her like a tide she couldn't control. For a fleeting second, she wondered what it would be like to lift the wrought iron lamp on the nightstand and bring it crashing down on his head. It seemed like a relatively easy way to kill someone. But then she would never find out who he had been unfaithful with. And, with every fiber of her being, she desperately wanted to know. She shook her head free of her macabre thoughts. She could never harm Brock. As pathetic as it was, she couldn't even imagine divorcing him for being unfaithful.

First things first, she needed to confirm her suspicions. She had little evidence to go on, so far. The text thread had consisted of only two messages. Anything prior to that had been deleted. If she confronted him, he might claim he'd only exchanged a couple of flirty texts. Inhaling a deep breath, she headed into the master bath to clean her teeth. Far better to arm herself with undeniable proof before she squared up to him. She would follow him next time he told her he was going golfing and see for herself who Brock was sneaking around behind her back with.

The next few days were almost unbearable as Ricki fought the urge to confront him about the jewelry receipt and the text messages she'd found on his phone—both of which she'd taken pictures of so there was no way he could deny their existence. If their marriage was over, she had to make sure to protect her interests. Each time she put her key in the door after returning home from work, dread curled its tentacles around her heart. It was proving more difficult than she'd envisioned to pretend everything was fine—not to mention pasting a fake smile on her lips as she greeted him. Worst of all, was when Brock touched her. It took every ounce of her willpower not to flinch and shove him aside.

"I need to go into the office for a few hours," she told him on Saturday morning.

"That's fine," he replied, barely lifting his gaze from his iPad.

"What are you going to do all day?" Ricki asked nonchalantly. "There's plenty of yard work that needs to be done if you're at a loose end."

Brock's brows bunched together in a frown. "Actually, I might play a round of golf while you're at the office. I can tackle the weeds this afternoon."

Ricki shrugged, trying to tamp down the sudden rush of adrenalin surging through her. She drained the last of her coffee and reached for her purse and keys. "I'll see you in a few hours."

She backed out of the garage and drove in the direction of *XCell-Nourish*, all the while keeping an eye on Brock's location on her iPhone *Find My Friends* App. As soon as she saw he was on the move, she pulled over and watched the screen for several minutes. He wasn't heading toward *Ridgecrest Golf Club* where Dave was a member. She sighed as she pulled back into the traffic and followed him from a distance. It was probably wishful thinking on her part that there might still be a possibility he was going to play golf at some other location. But she couldn't help keeping a flicker of hope alive as she drove.

Brock's Lexus came to a stop on an unfamiliar street in a part of town she'd never been to before. A few minutes later, she cruised slowly past his empty car, scoping out the situation. He'd parked on West Elm Street outside an inconspicuous apartment building in a shabby neighborhood. After leaving her BMW out of sight on a nearby street, she pulled a hat over her head and started back to the corner of West Elm to wait for Brock to reappear. Dressed in a shapeless overcoat she'd picked up at a thrift store, she was unrecognizable, even if he happened to glance down the street and spotted her loitering behind a leafy tree. She pulled a pair of binoculars out of her oversized purse and trained them on the apartment building. From her vantage point, she would be able to get a good look at anyone going in or out.

Minutes ticked by, and then, before she knew it, an entire hour had passed. Her feet were beginning to ache in her heels by the time the door to the apartment on the ground floor opened. Brock's familiar shape filled the doorway, his back blocking her view of the woman in the short skirt he was talking to. A rhythmic whooshing of blood flooded Ricki's eardrums. She wet her lips, her heart pounding painfully as she waited for Brock to move out of the way. If nothing else, at least she knew now where the tramp lived. A profound feeling of sadness gripped her as her worst fears materialized in front of her eyes. She watched Brock embrace the woman before turning to leave. A tiny sob escaped her lips. For a fleeting moment, she caught a glimpse of her replacement before the door to the apartment swung closed. Nausea rose up her throat. The woman was half her age—young, virile, and gorgeous.

Slowly, Ricki lowered her binoculars, resignation settling like a damp fog in her broken heart. She could no longer fool herself into hoping there might be a perfectly plausible explanation for the diamond ring and the stream of lies that went along with it. The cold hard facts were staring her in the face. Her husband of twenty-two years was cheating on her.

The only question jackhammering inside her brain now was what to do about it.

31

"Are you sure you're all right?" Maria asked, peering at Ricki across the conference table the following morning with a concerned look in her eyes. "You've scarcely said a word."

Ricki shuffled a few papers on the desk in front of her, averting her gaze. She'd come up with several good ideas to present at their monthly strategy meeting, but everything had blurred together in her brain the minute the meeting began. Her mind was elsewhere, mulling over Brock's infidelity and what to do about it. The thought of divorcing him terrified her. She didn't want to start over, or live alone, or have to put up with everyone at the office shooting her sympathetic looks when word got out that he'd been unfaithful. And then there was the financial fallout to consider. She had a stock option on the horizon, which could prove to be extremely lucrative. Would Brock be entitled to half of everything she'd worked so hard for?

By the same token, she couldn't envision remaining married to a man who was sleeping with another woman. Maybe there was a third option—an ultimatum. What if he was remorseful and agreed to end the affair? They could go to therapy, work things out—lots of couples did. "I'm sorry," she said, collecting herself. "I didn't sleep well last night. I'm running on empty this morning."

Maria and Ivy exchanged skeptical looks.

"Are you sure you're not coming down with something?" Ivy ventured. "You haven't been yourself for the past few days."

Ricki hesitated before answering. A part of her wanted to unload her fears and insecurities on Ivy and Maria and get their feedback. But the thought of them glimpsing the raw pain ravaging her heart paralyzed her. Even though she'd done nothing wrong, she was filled with embarrassment and shame at the thought of disclosing to her friends that Brock had been carrying on an illicit affair behind her back.

When Ivy and Jim had lost their daughter, Ivy had handled her grief privately. She'd taken off work for a couple of weeks and come back with renewed vigor, accepting her colleagues' condolences with grace and fortitude. She hadn't collapsed in on herself or sat sobbing at her desk. Ricki couldn't afford to show weakness. She'd already stumbled once this week. She'd learned this morning that the distributor she'd pitched to had declined to sign on with *XCellNourish*. Maria had little patience for failure. Ricki needed to project a competent, successful image and prove to her boss that she was capable of shouldering her responsibilities. She didn't trust herself not to break down if she opened up about her problems. Better to say nothing. She would decide what to do about Brock on her own.

With a bright smile, she reached for the sheaf of papers in front of her. "I'm fine. I just need a shot of coffee and I'll perk right up. I did have a couple of thoughts about our new marketing campaign." She passed each of them a copy of the ideas she'd roughed out earlier in the week. Willing herself to stay focused, she ran through her suggestions. Within minutes, Ivy and Maria were absorbed in the upcoming campaign, caught up in the excitement of a new product release to the market. With the spotlight off her, Ricki exhaled a silent sigh of relief. Brock's dirty little secret was safe, for now.

"Why don't you head home early today?" Maria suggested, when their meeting ended. "Put your feet up on the couch, watch a Netflix movie and kick back for once. You've earned it. We're not leaving for the lake until 5:00 p.m."

"I might do that," Ricki agreed, shooting her a grateful grin. "Probably better for my adrenals than shocking them with another round of caffeine."

"That's what's keeping you awake at night," Maria chided. "You should cut back. Better yet, stick to decaf. See you later. Don't forget to pack your swimsuit. We'll go wake surfing if the weather's good."

After locking up her office, Ricki made her way out to the parking lot and tossed her briefcase onto the passenger seat of her car. She started up the engine and then sat staring morosely through the windshield at the retaining wall in front of her. She didn't want to go home and watch some lame drama on Netflix. She was living through her own soap opera—a reality show she hadn't auditioned for. She'd been cast as one of those flat, cardboard characters who was simply there, like a piece of furniture to be used and abused at will. Curling her fists around the steering wheel, she gritted her teeth. She was sick and tired of being played like a fool. She couldn't put off confronting Brock any longer. She would have it out with him before they left for the lake.

But, first, she would pay his young mistress a visit and shake her up a bit. It was time someone set her straight on a few life lessons. She couldn't expect to waltz her way into another woman's marriage and take what didn't belong to her without any repercussions.

32

Ricki drove slowly to the east end of town and parked in the same spot she'd left her car when she'd followed Brock a few days earlier. She sat in the soft, leather seat for several minutes, going over in her mind what she intended to say to the woman Brock was cheating on her with. She was young and would likely break down in tears, but she needed to hear what Ricki had to say. She needed to understand the extent of the pain and destruction she'd caused by cavorting with a married man. The last thing she'd be expecting was for her lover's wife to appear on her doorstep. Ricki would have the element of surprise on her side, and she intended to use it to full advantage. It would be a trial run for her confrontation with Brock. If he was unwilling to end the affair, she would kick him out on the spot. He could find a hotel for the weekend for all she cared. After that, he would have to figure out a more permanent place to live. She wasn't going to allow him back into the house she was paying the mortgage on. After she'd had a few thousand words with his girlfriend, he might not be so welcome at her place anymore either.

Dressed in a smart power suit and designer black pumps, Ricki rounded the corner onto West Elm Street with a forceful stride, intent on taking command of the situation. She deserved better than to be made a fool of behind her back. Her confidence grew with every step she took. Judging by the apartment Brock's girlfriend lived in, she was far from a successful career woman. She would be no match for Ricki's years of experience. She would rip the woman to shreds verbally and relay a veiled threat to ensure she never came near Brock again.

Ricki slowed her pace as she approached the apartment door where she'd watched her husband locked in an embrace. The unsettling memory only strengthened her resolve. With any luck, the woman was home from work by now—that is, if she had a job at all. Ricki flattened her lips in distaste at the thought of the money Brock had spent indulging her with expensive gifts. He'd changed his credit card password, so she hadn't been able to log in to find out the full extent of his spending spree. He might even be paying the woman's rent, for all she knew. Little did they know that things were about to come crashing down around them in a big way.

Ricki took a deep breath before ringing the bell. She shifted impatiently from one foot to the other as she waited for the woman to come to the door. When no one appeared, she held her finger down on the bell, and then pressed it repeatedly, venting her frustration.

The door suddenly flung open, and a startled face stared out at her. For the briefest of moments, Ricki thought she detected a flicker of recognition in the woman's eyes. Ricki raised her brows, waiting for the woman to acknowledge her. Instead, she tightened a fluffy bathrobe around her waist and eyed Ricki up and down with an annoyed air. "If you're selling something, I'm not interested," she snapped, reaching for the door to slam it shut.

"*I'm* not the one who's selling something," Ricki shot back, jamming her foot in the door. "We need to talk. I believe you know my husband, Brock Wagner."

The woman pulled damp strands of dark hair back from her face, her eyes narrowing. "You're Ricki?"

"Mrs. Wagner to you."

The shock and awe effect Ricki was expecting her words to have never transpired. Instead, the woman's full lips curved into a cool smile brimming with predatory anticipation. "What can I do for you, *Mrs. Wagner?*"

"It would be best if we discuss that inside," Ricki said curtly.

The amused smile on the woman's face only deepened as she stepped aside with a flourish. "In that case, please come in."

Ricki followed the woman into a small kitchen outfitted with a few basic appliances. A pile of rumpled sheets was perched haphazardly on one end of the table next to an iron and a mug of steaming coffee. The woman reached for the mug and took a sip before locking her fingers around it and fixing her gaze on Ricki. She gestured with her chin to a chair. "Make yourself at home. I'm Tay, but maybe you already know that," she said, in a tone laced with amusement.

Ricki clenched her fists around the straps of her purse as she took a seat. So far, she wasn't making the imposing impression she'd envisioned. Instead of cowering in her presence, Tay was clearly enjoying trying to make her squirm. She had underestimated the girl's cockiness. Tay's utter indifference to the fact that her married lover's spouse had unexpectedly shown up on her doorstep was beyond infuriating. Ricki had visualized Tay groveling before her, sobbing and swearing she hadn't known Brock was married, promising to break it off and never to contact him again. The monologue she'd prepared in her head was rapidly dissolving in the acid bath of Tay's smug demeanor.

"Is Tay your real name, or just one you give your clients?" Ricki asked, arching a sharp brow.

Anger flickered momentarily in Tay's eyes, before a sickly-sweet smile parted her perfectly arched lips. "I can only imagine how difficult this must be for you, Mrs. Wagner. If I had to put myself in your shoes, I suppose it would be easier to believe that my husband's extramarital relationship was nothing more than a meaningless fling. But the truth is, Brock loves me." Tay sat down at the table, her green eyes glowing. She sank back in her chair and let out a satisfied chuckle. "It sounds cliche, but I never knew love like this existed. I thought it only happened in cheesy romance novels." She paused and pointed to her coffee mug. "How inconsiderate of me. Can I offer you something to drink?"

Ricki glared across the table at her. "How dare you patronize me! You can try all you want to undermine my marriage with your cheap shots, but it won't work. You can't wheedle your way into our lives. Brock and I have been together since we were nineteen. In all that time, my husband's love for me has never wavered. You're nothing to him, do you understand? Nothing!" She broke off abruptly at the quiver in her voice. She had wanted to keep her emotions from surfacing, but the enormity of the situation had crept up on her. Rage simmered inside, building to an intensity that was making her break out in a cold sweat. She wanted nothing more than to reach for Tay and slap her silly. She was only an impressionable girl caught up in the fantasy of an older man fawning all over her, plying her with gifts.

Tay pulled her bottom lip between her teeth and blinked pity-ingly at Ricki. "I can tell from your reaction that this comes as a shock to you. I'm sorry to break it to you like this, but Brock assured me you two were separated. He said your marriage had been disintegrating for some time now."

Ricki swallowed the jagged lump in her throat. Did he really see their marriage as doomed? Was it that far gone? She had surrendered to the status quo—their mundane exchanges as they entered and exited their home. She'd told herself it was understandable, accept-able even. That's what busy, successful people did. Everyone's life operated in the same manner nowadays—an exchange of sound bites while hunched over their phones. But it appeared Brock hadn't been so accepting of it. He'd replaced her with a younger, updated model.

"You're mistaken," she said briskly. "Misled might be a better word. My husband used you, but you mean nothing to him. He loves me."

Tay's gracefully shaped brows elevated a fraction. "I guess he hasn't told you, yet."

"Told me what?" Ricki demanded.

Tay frowned down at her coffee mug before lifting her eyes, a doe-like expression on her face. "He's divorcing you."

Ricki snorted. "And you believe that? What other line can a married man use to convince a woman half his age to jump into bed with him?"

Tay cleared her throat. "Mrs. Wagner, can I call you Ricki?" She went on without waiting for an answer. "Brock and I are engaged."

33

The words hit Ricki like a foul ball between the eyes. For a moment or two, her lips flapped, oddly disconnected from her brain, as she fought to formulate a response. Her thoughts flew in myriad directions, a cluster bomb of emotions detonating inside. She watched in silence as Tay set down her mug, reached into the pocket of her robe, and pulled out a sleek, black, velvet box. She popped it open and slipped a sparkling diamond ring on the fourth finger of her left hand. A perfect fit. Ricki's heart plummeted like a broken elevator in a horror movie. She'd been right all along about the jewelry receipt for a diamond. An engagement ring, no less.

Tay held out a slender hand to her and she shrank back in revulsion. The diamond winked mockingly up at her, its clarity and beauty belying the lies and deception it embodied.

Tay reached behind her and pulled open a cabinet drawer. She tossed a few brochures on the kitchen table and began to flick through them. "We've already been looking at honeymoon spots. I've always wanted to go to Fiji." She tinkled a laugh. "I had to buy a new suitcase. I've never traveled outside the US before."

"You're fooling yourself. You're not going anywhere," Ricki sputtered. "You may think you're engaged to Brock, but I'm married to the man. The ring's just to placate you. Don't you get it? He's using you."

Tay smiled admiringly down at the impressive stone on her finger. "Brock tells me you're a very busy woman. An important force at *XCellNourish*. It's taken over your life. Surely you can understand how he felt unloved and ignored."

"You don't know the first thing about my career!" Ricki snarled. "*Or* my marriage."

Tay arranged her lips into a sad pout. "Poor Mrs. Wagner. My heart breaks for you. I know more than you think. I know all about your infertility struggles. It must be devastating to be told you'll never carry a child. I mean a puppy's great and all, but let's face it, it's no replacement for a mini-Ricki or a Brock junior, is it?"

Ricki's eyes widened in shock. Tay couldn't possibly have known about her struggle to have a child unless Brock had told her. This was almost a worse betrayal than discovering he was sleeping with another woman. Tay was talking flippantly about her most intimate pain—the agony she and Brock had walked through together. He had seen inside to the deepest places of her broken heart. They had cried and mourned together, and then healed together through long years of therapy, finally coming to a place of acceptance. But it was not a journey they shared with anyone—it was their private path of pain.

Tears skated over Ricki's burning eyeballs. She blinked furiously to clear her vision, drowning in alternating waves of shame and rage. Brock had even told Tay about their decision to adopt a puppy instead of pursuing any more rounds of IVF. She felt violated on a whole other level at the thought of Brock and this tramp discussing her most intimate secrets. Did Brock resent all those years of trying for a child? Had he complained to Tay that he'd been forced to endure round after round of fertility treatments? A sudden flush crept over Ricki's cheeks. She felt exposed and naked in front of this stranger who had surreptitiously slipped like a serpent into her life and between her sheets.

"You look like you could use a stiff drink," Tay said, sliding the diamond ring from her finger and replacing it in its box. "Brock and I were just celebrating our engagement with some vodka tonics last night. I know there's some left." She got to her feet and set the velvet box on the kitchen counter. Opening a cabinet, she reached for a half full bottle of vodka, then deftly poured two shots. Ricki stared vacantly at the Grey Goose label on the side—Brock's favorite. He wasn't ordinarily a big drinker, but he enjoyed the occasional vodka tonic. A shiver of repulsion went through her at the thought of Tay knowing all these personal details about her husband, catering to his desires on every level.

Returning to the table, Tay set one of the glasses in front of Ricki and gave a sheepish shrug. "It's past five o'clock." She reached for her glass and downed it in one gulp.

Ricki stared numbly at the shot glass in front of her. She didn't like vodka but, right now, she could use a swig of something to summon her senses. She desperately needed to take control of this situation and steer the conversation in the direction she'd intended for it to take. Deep down, she knew Brock would never leave her. Tay was just a plaything on the side. She needed to understand that that was the extent of her role. She would never be Mrs. Wagner 2.0. Ricki reached for the vodka. She threw it back and slammed the glass down on the table. "Brock will never leave me for you. You're merely a diversion. I'm giving you fair warning. I'm going to go home and confront him after this, and give him an ultimatum, and then your little affair will be over, just like that." She snapped her fingers for emphasis. "You can cry all you want into that bottle of vodka, but he's not coming back. I love my husband and he loves me. I'll do whatever it takes to keep him." She cast a scathing glance around the room. "Keep the ring. Sell it and buy yourself some decent furniture. I don't care. Just stay away from my husband."

Tay gave a disbelieving shake of her head, twirling her shot glass slowly between her thumb and forefinger. "You really don't get it, do you Mrs. Wagner? Your marriage is over. Brock wants a life you can never give him." She leaned forward, tilting her head to one side like a therapist contemplating her patient. "All he's ever wanted is a child. And I can give him one."

34

Something snapped inside Ricki, fueling a brutish instinct. She leapt from the chair and flew at Tay, clawing at her with a ferocity she didn't know she possessed. "How dare you! You're nothing but scum! You'll never take Brock away from me!"

Tay screamed and stumbled backward against the kitchen counter, her frantic eyes locked on Ricki as her fingers groped around behind her. Ricki eyed the knife block just beyond Tay's reach. Her eyes widened when she realized what Tay was trying to grab hold of. She couldn't let her get to it—there was no telling what might happen if she got her hands on a blade. Grabbing hold of Tay's shirt, she tried to jostle her away from the counter.

"Get your hands off me! You're crazy!" Tay yelled, shoving her away from her. She flailed a hand frantically over the countertop, knocking the vodka bottle to the floor in her panicked state. The bottle smashed, strewing a glittering path of glass and liquid between them. Undeterred, Ricki crunched her way through it and grabbed Tay by the hair. "Don't you dare touch that knife!"

"You're insane!" Tay spat at her. "Let go of me!"

"I can see straight through you," Ricki said, sticking her face up close to Tay's. "You're nothing but a freeloader—profiting off other people's suffering. You have no intention of having a kid with my husband. You're milking him for all he's worth, and when you've had your fill of the fancy dinners and expensive jewelry, you'll walk away. Well guess what, it's my money you've been stealing."

"Let go of me, you ignorant cow!" Tay yelled. "You don't understand!"

"Oh, I understand all right. I understand that women like you are takers, here today and gone tomorrow. Brock and I have been together as long as you've been alive. We share a bond that someone as shallow as you will never be able to break."

The words had barely left Ricki's lips when she felt a stinging slap across her face. Momentarily stunned, she released her grip. Before she could regain her composure, Tay ducked beneath her and started for the door. She barely made it halfway across the tiny kitchen before Ricki got a hold of her flowing hair again and tugged her backward. Thrown off balance, she skidded in the stream of vodka and glass and landed with a sickening thump on the tile floor. Ricki stared down at her, her gaze flicking between the clump of dark hair in her fist and then back to the motionless body on the floor.

"Tay? Are you all right?" She stood there for several minutes, staring down at the unmoving form as shock seeped through her. Shaking, she knelt down next to Tay, vaguely aware of the sound of glass crunching beneath her. A dull throbbing pain registered in her knees. Her heart knocked against her ribs. "Tay, answer me!" she urged in a grating whisper. A ball of fear lodged in her throat as she waited for Tay to respond. She had a terrible feeling that something was wrong. Tay's eyes were wide open, and she was staring fixedly at a kitchen cabinet in the corner of the room. Ricki shook her by the shoulder, gently at first and then more insistently. "Tay! Tay, wake up!"

Her lips made no response, her body oblivious to Ricki's touch. Ricki patted the sides of her face frantically. "Tay, please wake up! I'm sorry! Groan or something. Just let me know you're okay. Please, please, please, be all right." Ricki rocked gently back-and-forth, her eyes never leaving Tay's expressionless face. Was this really happening? Tay looked like a China doll with her dark, damp curls strewn about her alabaster skin.

So young, so beautiful, so ... lifeless.

35

Ricki staggered to her feet and sank into a chair at the kitchen table. She'd checked for a pulse multiple times, hoping against hope that Tay's eyes would miraculously flutter open, and this nightmare would end. But it hadn't happened. It was unimaginable. How could Tay be dead? Ricki could barely breathe. If only she could rewind the last few minutes. If only she'd been able to keep her cool and handle herself like she did so effortlessly in the boardroom. The dressing down she'd planned to give Tay had gone horribly wrong. It was the callous mention of giving Brock a child that had triggered her unfettered rage—a rage born of disappointment and pain that was still raw despite the hours of therapy that only coated her emotions.

She stared forlornly at her empty glass. If Tay hadn't poured those shots of vodka, the bottle wouldn't have been out on the counter, and she'd never have smashed it and slipped. Ricki's gaze wandered down to the remnants of the etched Grey Goose glass strewn over the floor. No doubt Brock had bought the vodka. Why was she blaming herself for what had happened? This wasn't her fault. It wasn't Tay's fault either. It was Brock who was to blame for all of it. He'd deceived them both, his lies falling all too easily from lips that had told her a thousand times how much he loved her.

A thick sob squeezed its way up Ricki's throat and she buried her face in her hands. She felt as though she was hyperventilating. What was she going to do now? She couldn't call 911. She knew how this would look—scorned wife attacks husband's lover in a jealous rage. The minute law enforcement arrived on the scene she'd be led away in handcuffs. She'd only wanted to stop Tay attacking her with a kitchen knife. She'd never intended to kill her. She'd come here to scare her off, to reclaim her marriage. If anyone, it was Brock she wanted to hurt.

She plunged her hands despairingly into her hair. The right thing to do would be to call the police, but she didn't want to go to prison. She doubted even the most expensive lawyers would be able to save her from this mess. Best case scenario, she'd be tried for manslaughter, but it could be worse—much worse. The prosecution might argue that she'd planned all along to murder Tay. A sense of hopelessness engulfed her. There was a very real possibility she could spend the rest of her life behind bars, all because her husband's mistress had slipped in the vodka he'd bought to celebrate their engagement and hit her head. How was that her fault? It wasn't fair that she should have to pay the price for their infidelity. It was wrong on so many levels.

Ricki furrowed her brow in concentration. The steady thrumming of blood in her ears increased as she weighed her options. No one knew she was here. Brock had no idea she knew where Tay lived, or even that he'd been having an affair, for that matter. She'd parked her car on another street so no one would be able to tell the police they'd noticed a white BMW outside Tay's apartment building. If she could figure out a way to dispose of the body, and wipe the place clean, no one could connect her to this horrible accident, which was exactly what it amounted to.

She took a shallow breath, as she considered the idea. Maybe there was a way to make this all go away. She stared down at Tay's lifeless body, locking in her decision.

If she wasn't already a criminal, she was about to become one.

36

Ricki pulled out her phone and checked the time. She'd only been in Tay's apartment for twenty-five minutes. How could so much have possibly transpired in such a short span of time? A wave of panic rippled through her as the enormity of the task that lay ahead sank in. The first order of business was to find something to wrap the body in. She took a shaky breath and got to her feet, eying the short hallway that presumably led to the bedroom area. After a quick glance outside to make sure no one was around, she padded down the carpeted hall to Tay's bedroom. Her eyes darted frantically around the room, searching for a rug, or a blanket. She briefly considered pulling the sheets off the bed, but that would look suspicious. She couldn't afford to make those kinds of basic mistakes.

Slipping into the bathroom next door, she spotted a small linen closet. To her relief, she discovered several extra sets of sheets stacked inside. With shaking fingers, she removed an entire set, pillowcases and all. She knew from watching true crime shows that if only a single sheet was missing, it would arouse the suspicions of any investigator worth his salt. Armed with her rudimentary supplies, she headed back up to the kitchen, steeling herself to move the body. Tay was small and slender, but Ricki still struggled to maneuver her dead weight onto the sheets and roll her up inside. She stood and blew out a breath as she surveyed her handiwork. With a sinking feeling, she realized she'd accomplished little so far. It wasn't as if she could pick up Tay's body and carry it out to her car in broad daylight. Frowning, she racked her brain for a better idea. Her gaze landed on the colorful brochures still scattered across the table.

Retracing her steps to the bedroom, she opened the accordion doors to Tay's closet and dug around. Behind the shoe rack, she found a rose quartz colored suitcase with the price tag still attached. It was a fancy designer one with wheels that rotated in all directions, allowing it to glide easily. More important, it was big enough to fit Tay's body inside. Swallowing the bile gathering at the back of her throat, Ricki rolled the suitcase back down the hallway to the kitchen and laid it out flat next to Tay's shrouded form. It took some effort, but she managed to roll her into the suitcase and arrange her in a fetal position, before zipping the case closed.

Her breath came in short, sharp stabs as she stared down at the shiny new case that was about to become Tay's coffin. This was wrong. What was she thinking? There was still time to call the authorities. She could explain that she'd panicked in the moment, that she'd been in shock when she'd put Tay's body in the suitcase. Surely, they would be sympathetic once they heard the whole story. Forensic experts could prove that Tay had slipped in the vodka, couldn't they? She shook her head, knowing it was a lost cause. How would she explain why she was in the apartment to begin with? She could try all she wanted to convince herself that she would be acquitted of any wrongdoing, but if she was on a jury examining the evidence, she'd convict the scorned wife in a heartbeat.

An icy breath razored its way up her throat as she wheeled the suitcase to the front door and forced herself to focus her attention on cleaning up the kitchen. After donning a pair of rubber gloves she found beneath the sink, she loaded the shot glasses into the over-flowing dishwasher and set it to run. For the next hour-and-a-half, she worked diligently mopping up the spilled vodka with rags and vacuuming the glass. When she was done, she took a trash bag with the rags inside and set it next to the suitcase at the front door to dispose of later. Gingerly, she removed the vacuum bag and replaced it with a new one before returning the appliance to the cabinet where she'd found it. Next, she bleached the floor and wiped down every surface. Slowly, she surveyed the room, searching for any detail she might have overlooked. She should have been hot and sweaty after all that work, but instead she was cold—an ominous reminder that Tay's core body temperature was steadily dropping inside the case as death took hold.

Satisfied that she'd done a thorough job, Ricki made her way to the front door and frowned down at the suitcase and trash bag. She hadn't thought through the next part of her plan. Wheeling the suitcase all the way to her car was a bad idea. She ran the risk of passing people on the sidewalk, or someone driving by might notice her. The unusual color of the suitcase would stick in their mind if the police started asking questions. She needed to come up with a better alternative. A wave of despair descended, threatening to break her. Who was she kidding? She wasn't cut out for this. She wasn't a criminal. Even now, she could still change her mind and confess to what she'd done. She was only digging a bigger hole for herself as the minutes ticked by. Her eyes darted desperately around the apartment. The meticulous work she'd put in cleaning the place wouldn't bode well in a case against her. She'd gone too far already. There was nothing else for it but to finish what she'd started and dispose of Tay's body. And to do that, she somehow had to get it into the trunk of her BMW.

Her options were limited. It was too risky to bring her car around to Tay's apartment, but it was equally risky to drag the case all the way down the street and around the corner to where she'd parked. Perhaps Tay had a vehicle close by. If that were the case, she could dress up in Tay's clothes and wheel her suitcase out to her car without raising any suspicions. For the next few minutes, she searched the apartment, even emptying out Tay's purse, but the only key she found was for the front door. Frustrated, she tossed Tay's purse on the floor next to the suitcase. She would need to dispose of that along with the body. Twisting the apartment key between her fingers, she searched for another idea. She was running out of time. They were due to leave for the lake house at five o'clock.

She needed to make it look as if Tay had gone away on a trip. She could drive her BMW to the airport and then Uber back to Tay's apartment. From there she could hail another Uber—better still, a taxi or Lyft—and have them take her to the airport with Tay's luggage. If she donned one of Tay's hats and wore dark sunglasses, the driver wouldn't be able to identify her. If he was ever questioned, he'd think he'd picked up Tay and dropped her off at the airport. It was perfect—at least she hoped it was. It wasn't as if she had much experience in this sort of thing. Setting her lips in a grim line of determination, she reached for the trash bag, stuffed it into her oversized purse, along with the rubber gloves, and a couple of extra trash bags, and then exited the apartment to execute the first stage of her plan.

On the ride back to Tay's apartment from the airport an hour later, Ricki avoided striking up a conversation with the Uber driver by pretending to be busy on her phone. He looked young enough to be in high school and seemed more interested in grunting along to his rap music than conversing with her anyway. The straw hat she'd found in Tay's closet had proven perfect for concealing her face.

Safely back inside the apartment, she waited by the front door for a full fifteen minutes before calling for a Lyft. She needed to use the bathroom, but she wasn't about to pull out the bleach and go through the process of removing any trace of her DNA all over again. She'd been careful not to touch anything, even going so far as to use her sleeve to push open the front door after she'd unlocked it. Not that her fingerprints were on file in any criminal databases, but it was better to be overly cautious. She'd return the housekey to Tay's purse and zip it inside the suitcase later. A shudder ran through her at the thought of opening it back up. At least Tay was wrapped inside the sheets, and she wouldn't have to look at her face.

By the time the Lyft driver arrived, Ricki's nerves were frayed to threads. Her throat was parched, and she berated herself for not staying hydrated. She hadn't eaten anything since breakfast either—

hopefully, she didn't pass out. After nonchalantly wheeling the suitcase out to the waiting car, she attempted to lift it into the trunk.

"Let me help you with that," the driver offered. He grabbed a corner and together they shoved the case into the trunk.

"You don't pack light, do you?" the driver laughed, before jumping in behind the wheel.

"I'm going overseas for a couple of months," Ricki replied tersely.

"Nice! What terminal are we off to?"

"United." Ricki promptly pulled out her phone and dialed her bank's number, knowing she would get a recording. She proceeded to conduct a conversation with an imaginary person on the other end of the line. Taking the hint, the driver turned his attention back to a podcast he was listening to.

The minute they reached the departures terminal, Ricki jumped out to grab the suitcase. She yanked it to the ground, waving off the driver's offer of assistance and then headed inside. As soon as the Lyft driver disappeared from view, she exited the terminal and walked across to the short-term parking garage where she'd left her car. Before loading the suitcase into her BMW, she carefully lined the trunk with the extra trash bags. She couldn't afford to risk any leakage from her cargo. Huffing and puffing, she finally managed to shove the suitcase into the trunk. It was a lot harder getting it in than pulling it out. She hurried around to the driver's side, slid behind the wheel, and locked her car. Sweating profusely, she glanced at herself in the rearview mirror, flinching at the foreign eyes staring back at her.

There was no coming back from the dark place she'd gone. Somehow, she was going to have to drive up to the lake house later this afternoon and act as if everything was normal. She couldn't tell anyone what she'd done—she could scarcely believe it herself. Maria and Ivy would never in a million years believe she was capable of such a depraved act. And it wasn't over yet. She still had to dispose of Tay's body. Frowning, she stared vacantly through her windshield at the graffitied wall of the parking garage. Time slipped away as her mind churned through several unappealing options. She didn't have time to bury the body, and she couldn't risk unloading the suitcase in a dumpster in broad daylight. She would have to take it to a deserted location and ditch it—somewhere in the woods would be best.

The sharp trill of her phone startled her out of her reverie. Brock's number came up on the screen. Her skin crawled at the thought of talking to him, knowing Tay's body was in the trunk of her car. She let the call go to voicemail and started up the engine. Her eyes widened as she stared at the clock on her console in disbelief. *Quarter after four.* How was that possible? She'd been moving way more slowly than she'd realized. There was no time now to drive out to the forest to dump the suitcase. Her plan had been to leave it in a hollow and toss some leaves and debris over it. Inevitably, it would be discovered at some point—her hope being that the police would assume Tay had been abducted on her way to the airport and her body dumped in the woods. She didn't want to think too much more about it. It was an undignified way to dispose of Tay's remains, but it wasn't as if she'd be able to dig a hole big enough to bury her body without a shovel.

Sweat beaded along Ricki's forehead as she accelerated and merged with the traffic exiting the airport. What should she do? If she called Maria and told her she would be arriving at the lake house later than planned, she would have to come up with a good reason why. It was important not to arouse any suspicions by changing her timeline. Even the smallest detail could betray her. She didn't want to go to prison. She had no choice but to hurry home and leave with Brock at five as planned—not quite as planned.

Tay would be going with them.

37

"Where on earth have you been? I've been trying to call you," Brock grumbled, when Ricki pulled up outside the house. "I thought we were supposed to be leaving at five. I got home an hour ago."

"It's only two minutes past," Ricki said curtly. Her legs trembled as she climbed out of the car.

Brock threw her a disgruntled look and followed her into the house. "First, you ignore my calls and then you show up at the last minute and bite my head off. I can see we're going to be in for a great weekend."

If only you knew. Ricki fixed a steely gaze on him. "Did you lock the doors and windows?"

"Already taken care of."

"What about the garden shed?"

"Seriously?" Brock shook his head. "Who do you think's going to be prowling the neighborhood stealing lawnmowers in our absence?"

"Just do it and quit griping," Ricki snapped. Her heart hammered a frenzied beat beneath her ribs. Would she even be able to keep it together until they got to the lake?

Brock scowled. "You really are in a foul mood. I don't know why you're taking it out on me. You must have had a rotten day at work or something. You're not going to be like this all weekend, are you? Because if you are, I'd rather stay behind."

"Let me guess, you'd rather be playing golf?" Ricki shot him an icy glare and then stomped up the stairs. It was going to take every ounce of her willpower this weekend to pretend to Maria and Ivy that everything was all right, but she had no intention of playing nice with Brock on the drive up to the lake. She had too much on her mind— the most pressing of which was how to dispose of Tay's body. After that, she would decide if her marriage could be saved.

She took a few minutes in the bathroom to freshen up, then grabbed her overnight bag from the bedroom and made her way back downstairs. Peering through the kitchen window, she spotted Brock at the bottom of the garden wrestling with the padlock on the shed. She couldn't care less if it was locked or not, she'd just needed to get rid of him briefly so she could catch her breath. She reached for his duffel bag lying in the hallway and carried it out to her car. Her stomach roiled as she tossed both their bags onto the back seat. At all costs, she had to make sure Brock didn't open the trunk for any reason. She squeezed the key fob in a death grip in her hand as she slid behind the wheel to wait for him. It was only an hour's drive to the lake—not enough time for a decomposing body to begin to smell. But it wouldn't take long. She would have to dispose of it tonight.

The drive up to the cabin was tense, interspersed with petty bickering over nothing in particular. It was on the tip of Ricki's tongue, more than once, to confront Brock about the affair, but she knew she would be implicating herself in a horrific crime if it all came tumbling from her lips. Not to mention the fact that she couldn't predict how Brock would react to the shocking news that Tay was dead, and that her body was in the trunk. Would he even believe her that it had been an accident? What if he flew into a murderous rage and they ended up driving off the side of the road into the river? He made a few attempts, along the way, to ask her what was bugging her, but she played it off as a bad day at work and, eventually, he nodded off.

When they finally pulled up outside Maria's lake house, Ricki took a deep breath to fortify herself. She'd made it this far. She only had to fake it for a few more hours until everyone went to bed and then she could dispose of Tay's body under the cover of darkness. Pasting a stiff smile on her face, she waved back at Maria who was standing by the front door waiting to greet them.

"Grab the bags from the back seat," Ricki said to Brock.

Wordlessly, he reached in and pulled them out, a resigned expression on his face.

Ricki pressed the key fob, the reassuring beep letting her know the car was locked.

Brock raised his brows. "What are you locking it for? It's perfectly safe here."

"You know I'm fastidious about locking my BMW," Ricki said in a tone of admonishment. "You can never be too careful."

"Yeah, some drifter might climb in during the night and be waiting to cap us in the morning," Brock scoffed.

Ignoring him, Ricki marched over to the front door and embraced Maria with as much enthusiasm as she could muster up.

Fortified with a seemingly bottomless supply of margaritas, the three couples mingled on the back deck while Alex grilled their steaks. Ricki pretended to sip on her drink, discreetly disposing of the contents of her glass on her frequent trips to the bathroom. She needed to keep a level head to accomplish what she had to do tonight. She avoided meeting Brock's gaze whenever he threw a pained look her way, deliberately seating herself on the other side of the fire pit from him. As the evening wore on, and the group became tipsy, she struggled to keep up a lighthearted conversation. From time to time, she tentatively sniffed the air, half-afraid the odor of decomposing flesh might already be wafting toward the back deck, even though she'd parked in the shade and the sun had long since set.

By now, she'd lost count of how many margaritas the others had consumed. Jim, in particular, had gotten rowdy and loud. Maria's neighbor, Larry, had even called the police on them at one point to complain about the noise. They were fading now, stifling yawns as the jawing and laughter began to lag. Taking no chances, Ricki had slipped a handful of sleeping pills into the jug of margarita she'd carried out to the patio for Alex earlier. The last thing she needed was for one of them to wake up in the middle of the night and spot her struggling to the end of the dock with a suitcase in tow.

During the course of the evening, she'd decided that dumping Tay's body in the lake was the best option open to her. She would weigh it down with some rocks and hope for the best that it sank. She should probably have done some research on the topic, first, but time hadn't been on her side. It wasn't as good a plan as abandoning the body in the woods on the way to the airport, but it was the best she could come up with, given the circumstances. If the body was discovered, it would be a kind of poetic justice that the obvious suspect would be Brock.

Ricki sucked in a jagged breath when the group finally broke apart and bid each other goodnight. A little before 3:00 a.m., she gingerly turned back the covers and sat upright on the edge of her bed. She waited for a minute or two, barely breathing as she listened to her husband's rhythmic snoring. The sound was achingly familiar, yet, she felt as if she barely knew the man who had betrayed her in the worst possible way. He shifted in his sleep, letting out a soft, fluttering sigh. Ricki tensed, wondering if he was reveling in some dream featuring Tay. Little did he know that his dreams would be the only time he would be able to enjoy her from now on. Rising to her feet, Ricki crept across the wooden floorboards, conscious of every creak and movement. Unfamiliar with the idiosyncrasies of Maria's cabin, and desperate not to wake anyone, it took her what seemed like forever to cross the room. She reached for the dark sweats and hoodie she'd left draped on a chair and padded into the bathroom to dress.

Armed with only her key fob and her phone, she made her way quietly down the stairs at an agonizingly slow pace. She didn't dare let her thoughts wander to the body in the trunk of her car. If she allowed herself to dwell on the reality of what she was about to do, she might back out—a move that would mean spending the rest of her life in prison. She hesitated for a moment at the front door, trying to remember what Maria had said about the alarm. She had given them all the code earlier, but Ricki was almost certain she'd said they didn't bother setting the alarm when they were there. She turned on the flashlight on her phone and held it up to the panel on the wall to read the screen. *Disarmed.* Slowly, she released her breath. One less thing to worry about on her way back in.

Inch by inch, she opened the front door and then carefully closed it again behind her. Satisfied that she'd made it outside without waking any of the occupants of the house, she darted down the steps and across the gravel driveway to her car. Adrenalin was pumping through her, igniting every cell in her body. The next few minutes required more speed than stealth. She needed to get that suitcase into the lake as quickly as possible. If she was caught wheeling it down the dock, it would be impossible to explain away what she was doing, but if she was intercepted on the way back into the house, it would be a different story. She could simply say she hadn't been able to sleep and wanted to see the moonlight on the lake, or something equally benign. After a quick glance around to make sure no one was watching, she pressed the key fob. The beep seemed to reverberate through the night like a fire alarm. She quickly hunkered out of sight behind the car, her fist curled around her key fob, as she waited for someone to stumble out of the house thinking one of the cars had been broken into.

When no one appeared, she transferred her attention to the wall of Ponderosa pines that separated Maria's cabin from her neighbor's. Was it possible Larry had heard the sound of the car trunk opening? Sound seemed to travel up here on the mountain, and especially around the water. If he slept with the window open, there was a chance he might have heard her. But what would he do about it? He was hardly going to get out of bed in the middle of the night to investigate. The trees were blocking his view anyway—he'd have to walk all the way down his driveway to the main road and up the lane to Maria's house to see anything.

After talking herself down off the ledge, Ricki began the arduous process of removing the case from the back of her BMW. It seemed heavier than she remembered. A horrifying vision flashed to mind of the case falling to the ground and popping open, and Tay's body spilling out, her face pale as marble under the moonlight, her eyes daggers of condemnation. Ricki gritted her teeth, willing herself to keep it together and get the job done. Grunting, she tugged the case inch-by-inch over the plastic she'd draped over the lip of the trunk, recoiling at the scraping noise it made. For one irrational moment, she hesitated, imagining it was the sound of Tay's fingernails reaching through the zipper and clutching at the plastic bumper. She quickly shook herself free of the disturbing thought. *She's dead, Ricki!*

With the suitcase finally on the ground, she closed the trunk and took a calming breath. The hardest part came next, weighing the case down. She shone the light from her phone along the edge of the gravel driveway looking for some decent-sized rocks. After gathering a small pile the size of baseballs, she knelt by the case, and reluctantly yanked the zipper open. Without looking at the contents, she pushed the rocks inside and quickly closed it back up again. It was time to finish this gruesome task. After it was done, she could fall apart.

She got to her feet and began pulling the case across the gravel driveway to the grassy embankment that led down to the dock. She hadn't anticipated it being so difficult to navigate the terrain, and the extra weight of the rocks wasn't helping. The suitcase's tiny wheels churned through the gravel at a snail's tempo, as resistance built. Several times, she was forced to stop and heave the case up and over the gravel to free it. When she finally reached the embankment, she took a moment to catch her breath, eying the house behind her for any signs of movement. The wheels of the case wobbled precariously as she continued her ghoulish trek toward the water. Guilt threatened to derail her, the dock stretching out like a reproving finger in the oily blackness of the water.

She shivered, trying not to imagine what would happen to Tay's body in its final resting place. She couldn't stand the idea of fish nibbling on her decaying corpse. She was counting on the suitcase staying closed when she tipped it into the lake. Until now, Ricki had avoided thinking about Tay's immediate family. It was too unbearable to picture her mother staring out of her window, wondering what had happened to her daughter, hoping one day Tay would reappear. Families of crime victims always said the *not knowing* was the worst part. Ricki moaned and tugged the suitcase harder. She had to get this over with before she chickened out.

With a valiant final push, she reached the dock and pulled the suitcase onto the wooden slats. She took a couple of steps and then froze at the loud, clattering of the wheels echoing through the stillness of the night. She tried lifting the case, but she'd already tweaked her back and there was no way she could carry it all the way to the end of the dock with the additional weight of the rocks. She supposed she could toss the suitcase over the side right where she stood. The idea was tempting, but she was too close to the shore. She needed to get to the end of the dock where the lake fell off quickly to depths of forty feet or more.

It was her best chance of ensuring Tay's remains wouldn't be discovered—hopefully ever.

38

PRESENT DAY

A stony silence descended as Palmer's words sank in: *We've charged your husband in the murder of Tay Nicholson.* Ricki dipped her head into her hands, feigning the heartbroken reaction she knew was expected of her. Now that the bombshell had dropped, she wasn't sure what she felt. If anything, she was numb. In a way, it was a fitting end to the heinous saga, and not entirely unexpected. She'd known all along that Brock would be a suspect if Tay's body was discovered. After all, they'd been staying at the lake house that same weekend—and he'd lied to the police about not knowing Tay. And hidden the affair from her. Ricki shuddered, picturing what lay ahead. She dreaded all of it—the shame, the publicity, the guilt. *Guilt.* She hated that word. It churned constantly in her gut like a monster from the deep. But was it so wrong that Brock be held liable for Tay's death? He was responsible for triggering the disastrous series of events that had ended in tragedy. No doubt, he would plead not guilty, and the police had no real evidence to convict him. Still, given all the lies he'd told, he would have a tough time convincing a jury that he wasn't Tay's killer.

Ricki looked up and blinked at Palmer, reminding herself to play the part of the loving wife. "I ... I don't believe it. Just because Brock had an affair, it doesn't mean he's a murderer. He wouldn't hurt a fly." She wrung her hands in her lap. "Are you sure she was murdered? Brock doesn't have a violent bone in his body. He's never laid a finger on me."

"I know this comes as a shock." Palmer exchanged a loaded look with Lopez. "I can give you a few minutes alone with him if you like."

"Thank you," Ricki sniveled. "I'll talk to him. I'm sure this is all just a huge misunderstanding." She muttered to herself as she got to her feet, feigning utter bewilderment about the situation.

Palmer led her down the corridor and into another interview room with the same layout as the one she'd exited a moment earlier. She sank down at the table and stared across at Brock. She barely recognized him as her husband. His face had taken on a grayish tone and the eyes that met hers were sunken, empty orbs. She curled her hands into fists in her lap, trying to squeeze the pity from her soul. He had brought this suffering on himself—on both of them. He had destroyed everything.

Fighting her revulsion, Ricki reached across the table and laid a hand on his. "How are you doing?" she whispered.

"I'm fine." He squeezed her hand lightly in return. "It's you I'm worried about."

"I'm not the one sitting here in handcuffs," she said, gesturing to his wrists.

He sighed and shook his head sadly. "I don't blame them for suspecting me. I deserve it."

And then some! Ricki frowned. "Don't say that, honey. You were just in the wrong place at the wrong time. They can't hold you without any evidence."

"You don't understand. I brought this on myself."

Ricki leaned back in her chair and cocked her head to one side, anticipating a long-awaited confession. She had spent sleepless nights picturing this. He would tell her how deeply he regretted the affair, offer to go to therapy, and tearfully beg for her forgiveness. "What do you mean, you brought it on yourself?"

Brock searched her face as though evaluating whether or not she could handle what he was about to unload. "Did the police show you the photo of me and Tay?"

Ricki swallowed the lump in her throat, the sting of tears reminding her how close she was to the edge of breaking down. Even now, after everything, she still loved him. It tore her apart inside to know that Brock had cheated on her. The rejection was like a knife twisting deep in her gut. They were both about to pay a heavy price for what he'd done, but she was going to miss him. Learning to live without him would not come easy. But there was no turning back now from the part she'd played in sealing his fate. "Yes, Palmer showed it to me," she whispered, blinking furiously as a traitorous tear spilled onto the metal table and splattered between them.

"Please don't cry, babe!" Brock said. "I'm so sorry. I've been so stupid. If I could take it all back, I would."

"No more lies, Brock," Ricki said tersely. "I need you to tell me everything." The photo of him with Tay was evidence enough of his betrayal, but she still needed to hear him confess with his own lips what he'd done. Not that it would change anything, but at least he would finally come clean. Hearing him spell out the sordid details of his affair might even help quell her guilt, to some degree, about letting him take the fall for Tay's death.

Brock bunched his brows together and let out a heavy breath. "I've been hiding something from you, Ricki. I'm not proud of how I handled things. I should have come to you right away."

She fixed an icy gaze on him. "Go on."

He swallowed hard, his gaze meeting hers and then dropping to his handcuffed wrists on the metal table. "I have a daughter—*had* a daughter."

Ricki stiffened in the hard plastic chair, harpooned in position by the startling words. Her thoughts felt like they were exploding into dust in her brain as she scrambled for a response. "What ... what do you mean ... a daughter?"

Brock shook his head sadly. "Honey, Tay Nicholson was my biological daughter. She contacted me a few months ago, she tracked me down through ancestry.com. I didn't believe her, at first, so I did a paternity test. She was definitely mine." He paused and let out a shuddering sigh. "It was a one-night stand in college, the year before you and I met, a girl called Liv. I never saw her again. I never even knew about the pregnancy. When Tay first got in touch with me, I didn't know how to break the news to you. I wanted to take some time to think it through, first. I knew the heavy toll the miscarriages took on you—how much you wanted a child of your own. I didn't want to trigger another breakdown." He smiled forlornly across at her, interpreting her silence as sadness and not mute shock.

"Unfortunately, I realized pretty quickly that Tay hadn't tracked me down out of any real desire for a relationship with her biological father. She wanted money. She was extremely manipulative. She felt that I owed her for the lousy childhood she'd endured with a single mom whose boyfriend molested her—at least, that's what she claimed. She said she'd cut off all contact with her mother. I'm not sure how much of what she told me to believe. I found out some things about the circles she moved in that were pretty concerning. She pretended to want my fatherly love and affection, but all she really wanted was the stuff she pestered me to buy for her. She was cold and ruthless, playing on my emotions while pretending to be desperate for my love." Brock sighed, letting his shoulders sag. "Looking back, I think she was trying to punish me, in a way. I felt guilty that I hadn't been there for her, so I acquiesced to her demands. She even talked me into buying an engagement ring she wanted so her boyfriend could propose to her." Brock paused, as if trying to come to terms with his naïveté. "Dumb, I know. There was no boyfriend, as I found out later. She worked for a loan shark, and she only wore the ring to give the impression to potential clients that she was wealthy."

"Stop!" Ricki squeezed the word out, her throat aching from the growing lump threatening to block off her air supply.

"I know this is hard to hear—"

"I said, stop!" Ricki screamed at him, thumping a fist on the table.

Brock's brows shot up in alarm. "Honey, take it easy!"

Ricki staggered to her feet and looked across at Palmer who was observing the proceedings with an unreadable expression. "I ... I don't feel well."

Palmer swiftly got to his feet and placed a hand under her elbow as he guided her out of the room. "Restrooms are on the left," he said, pointing down the corridor.

Ricki shoved open the heavy metal door, feeling as if the walls were closing in on her. She could feel her body and mind slipping into full blown panic mode. A kaleidoscope of terrifying emotions whirled around inside her head. This couldn't be happening. It simply couldn't be true. It was a devious trick by the police to get her to confess. She had to stay strong. She bent over the sink and splashed cold water on her face with trembling fingers. Gasping as it stung her skin, she straightened up and stared at her reflection in the mirror. Slowly, she mouthed the four words of condemnation haunting her: *I have a daughter*. Her thoughts flashed back to the strange messages she'd discovered on Brock's phone: *D* for daughter. It all made sense now. She pressed a fist to her lips, trying to hold it together, but the tears came hot and heavy. Brock hadn't been unfaithful. He *loved* her. He'd always loved her.

A wave of horror washed over her, rocking her to her core. What had she done? She flattened her cold palms against her cheeks, trying to remember the details of Tay's face. How could she not have known? How could she not have seen a resemblance? But nothing about the petite, dark-haired young woman with the high sculpted cheekbones and sea-green eyes had reminded her of Brock.

Ricki clutched the edge of the porcelain sink, allowing herself to indulge in the fantasy that Tay could have been the daughter they'd always longed for—filling their lives with recitals and soccer games, perhaps even grandchildren. *No!* She ripped a paper towel from the holder and patted her face dry, squashing the illusion. The reality was that Tay had been a conniving gold digger who had no scruples when it came to milking people out of their hard-earned cash. She'd succeeded in taking their money, and she'd managed to destroy their lives in the process. She'd even taken a twisted delight in feeding into

Ricki's misperception that Tay was Brock's lover. Tay had allowed the monstrous lie to stand that had killed her.

Now, either Brock was going to prison for something he hadn't done, or Ricki would go to prison for something she hadn't meant to do.

39

That night, Ricki kept waking up gasping for air, feeling like she was drowning. In all her nightmares, she was sinking to the bottom of the lake in a suitcase weighed down with rocks, crying out for her mother. The full horror of what she had done was only now beginning to hit her. She'd been operating in a robotic state of shock when she'd come up with the plan to hide Tay's body. Afterward, she'd justified her actions based on the fatal misconception that Tay had seduced her husband. Now, she was forced to come to terms with the truth. She was appalled at the thought of the role she'd played in the death of Brock's child. Not to mention the cowardly way she'd covered it up, which had led to her husband being arrested on suspicion of murder. A preposterous charge. Brock was no murderer—he wasn't even an adulterer, as it turned out.

The medical examiner had ruled out drowning, but surely he couldn't prove that Tay had been murdered. She could have slipped and hit her head on the dock, for all anyone knew. It would be impossible to convict Brock on such flimsy evidence. A shiver ran across Ricki's shoulders at the thought of what he must be going through in police custody. She had to get him out of there. She pulled the comforter up to her neck and stared up at the ceiling, too sickened by her nightmares to risk closing her eyes again.

Shortly before 6:00 a.m. she made her way downstairs and turned on the Nespresso machine. She chewed the inside of her mouth as she agonized over the decision that lay ahead of her. She was still slumped in a chair in the kitchen, dressed in her robe and slippers, when Maria and Ivy came to the door a couple of hours later. They'd insisted on coming over as soon as they got wind of Brock's arrest.

"How are you doing?" Maria asked, enveloping her in a heartfelt hug.

Ricki shrugged as she led the two women back to the kitchen. "Hanging in there. It feels like I'm in a nightmare I can't wake up from."

She pottered over to her Nespresso machine and made Maria and Ivy a latte each. They sat around the kitchen table in silence for several moments before Ivy spoke up. "You know, I was so sure Jim had done it. When I heard about that photograph of Emily and Tay, I had a sinking feeling he might have tracked her down." She laced her fingers around her mug, frowning. "I never would have believed Brock was capable of something like this."

"He didn't do it," Ricki replied in a half whisper. "They've arrested the wrong person."

Maria raised her brows. "You don't think, Alex—" she broke off, a stricken look on her face. "I know he took the money from the company to settle his debts, but maybe Tay and this Levi guy wanted more. Alex might have panicked and done something stupid."

Ricki fought to keep her composure. It was hardly fair to let Maria suspect her own husband, but the alternative was no better. "All I can tell you is that Brock is a good man. He wouldn't kill his ... his own daughter."

"Daughter?" Ivy echoed in a hushed tone. "What are you talking about?"

Ricki reached up and wiped a dangling tear from her lashes. "All this time I thought Brock was having an affair, but I was wrong. Tay was his biological daughter. He had a one-night stand in college—he says he didn't know about the pregnancy. Tay found him through ancestry.com." Ricki pulled a tissue from her robe pocket and blew her nose. "She wasn't interested in finding her father, she was a gold digger. She wanted compensation. She guilted Brock into giving her money and buying her gifts to make up for the miserable life she claims she had with her druggie mother and her abusive boyfriend. She was manipulative and conniving, and the more Brock got to know her, the more he didn't want her in our lives. He was trying to figure out a way to tell me when ... well, you know."

Ivy and Maria stared at her, aghast.

"I can't believe it," Maria finally said, shaking her head in disbelief.

"You can't tell Jim that Tay was Brock's daughter," Ivy said in an urgent tone. "He thinks she's to blame for Emily's death. He might turn on Brock instead. He's beside himself that he didn't get to confront Tay." She frowned and bit her lip. "At least, that's what he's telling me. But if Brock didn't do it, maybe Jim got to her, after all."

Ricki squeezed her eyes shut and shook her head. "You mustn't think like that."

"Jim's going to find out that Tay was Brock's daughter, whether you tell him or not," Maria said. "It will all come out in the trial anyway."

A sob slipped through Ricki's lips.

"Oh, honey. I'm so sorry," Maria said, turning to Ricki with a pained expression on her face. "Forgive me. I wasn't thinking. It may not even come to a trial. Look, you just need to find Brock the best lawyer out there. If he didn't do this, there won't be any evidence to convict him. It's all circumstantial. The case will be dismissed. Worst case scenario, he'll be acquitted."

"The jury won't buy it," Ricki said, squeezing her hands together. "There are too many coincidences. Unless someone else comes forward and confesses, Brock's going to prison."

Maria was quiet for a moment. "I might as well tell you both now, I've asked Alex to move out. I can't trust him, not after stealing from the company. He's an addict and a liar, and if I find out he had anything at all to do with Tay's death, I'll turn him in myself."

Ricki's phone vibrated on the kitchen counter, interrupting their conversation.

Ivy got up and glanced at the screen. "It's Palmer. Do you want to take it?"

Ricki nodded resignedly. "He's probably calling to tell me which jail they transported Brock to. He said I can see him once he's booked in. I need to bring him a few things from home."

Ivy passed her the phone and Ricki slid her finger across the screen to accept the call.

"Hello," she said, flatly.

"It's Detective Palmer. Brock's been transferred to Northern Springs Correctional Center. You can visit him there this afternoon between the hours of three and four."

"Thank you," Ricki responded, recoiling inwardly at the thought of seeing her nerdy engineering husband in prison garb.

"I also wanted to let you know that an arraignment hearing has been set for Thursday."

Ricki closed her eyes briefly, a wave of nausea passing through her. It had suddenly become real. "Isn't there still a chance the judge will throw out the case? I mean, there's no real evidence a crime was even committed—Tay could have hit her head and fallen into the lake."

Palmer sighed. "You're going to see it on the evening news tonight anyway, so you might as well hear it from me. "A dive team retrieved a suitcase from Tamarack Creek Lake—close to where Tay's body was discovered. DNA testing confirms that she was in it, at some point." He hesitated for a moment as though willing her to grasp the significance of what he was saying.

"I'm sorry, Ricki, but she didn't climb into that suitcase and push it off the dock herself."

40

Ricki arrived at the correctional facility at exactly 2:50 p.m. She had looked over the list of items prisoners were allowed in their cells and packed a small bag of essentials for Brock, telling herself it would only be temporary. She grabbed the bag from the back seat and climbed out, her stomach sinking as she took in the maze of barbed wire, concrete walls, and metal fencing. Brock didn't belong in here. You had to be calloused, inside and out, to survive in a place like this. He was the sensitive sort. It would kill him. And she had put him here.

The irony was that she'd pictured Brock behind bars—wanted it, even—but that was back when she'd believed he was having an affair with Tay. It had seemed fitting that he would take the fall for her death as punishment for his betrayal. The revelation that Tay was actually his daughter still nauseated her every time she thought about it. Her fingers shook as she clutched the small bag of toiletries and sundries in her hand. She should be the one locked up in here, not Brock. She had killed his child and ruined all of their lives—in one form or another. She'd been right that he'd been lying to her but, in her haste, she'd jumped to the wrong conclusion. Confronting Tay before she'd confronted Brock had been a deadly miscalculation.

Ricki passed through the visitor screening in a catatonic stupor. In her mind, she went over everything she wanted to say to Brock in the short time they would have together. She had to persuade him to fight the charges with everything he had. She would hire the best lawyer to defend him, no matter the cost—she'd already put in several calls based on recommendations from Maria. No jury could convict him without any real evidence. A tiny thread of dread needled its way into her mind as she considered the alternative. If Brock was acquitted, would the trail lead to her? She shook herself free of the thought. No one knew she had confronted Tay in her apartment, or that she'd even suspected Brock was having an affair prior to his arrest. She was not in any danger. She had to focus her attention on getting Brock out of the mess she had put him in.

Seated at a small metal table in the visitors' area, Ricki picked nervously at her fingers as she waited for Brock to be brought into the room. Her heart jolted in her chest when she caught sight of him shuffling toward her in a rumpled orange jumpsuit. His hair was sticking up in haphazard clumps and mottled bags bulged beneath his eyes.

She attempted a weak smile as he sank down in the chair opposite her. "Hey! How are you holding up?"

He grimaced. "Okay. How are you?"

"I'm fine." She lowered her voice and leaned across the table. "Listen, Brock, I know you didn't kill Tay. We're going to fight these charges. I'll find you a good lawyer—the best there is. I already have an appointment lined up to meet with a candidate this afternoon. He's expensive, but Maria assures me he's worth every penny."

Brock shrugged disinterestedly. "I deserve this."

"Prison?" Ricki gave an indignant shake of her head. "You don't belong here. Of course you don't deserve this!"

"Lies and deception put me here."

Ricki sucked in a sharp breath. There was more truth to that statement than he realized—if only he knew it was her lies and deception that had handcuffed him. "You can't just give up! The police have no evidence against you."

Brock drew his brows tightly together. "Did you hear they found a suitcase at the bottom of the lake?"

Ricki stiffened. "I believe Palmer mentioned something about it."

"A suitcase weighted down with rocks." Brock hesitated and looked at her with something akin to pity. "It contained Tay's DNA."

Ricki took a shallow breath. She could hear the pounding of her heart beneath her blouse. "It doesn't prove anything."

Brock leaned across the table and whispered, "I recognized that case when they showed me a picture of it. I bought it for her."

Ricki shifted uncomfortably in her seat. "What difference does that make? You didn't put her in it."

Brock took a deep breath before responding. "That night at the lake house, I went back out to the car to look for my hiking boots. I had set them out by my duffel bag to bring with me. I thought you might have thrown them in the trunk or something. That's when I saw the case. At the time, I didn't think anything of it. I figured you'd packed it for a business trip the following week." He paused and dropped his gaze, his voice trailing off into a faint whisper. "Whatever happened, you can tell me, Ricki. I've always been your safe space."

Her mouth went dry. For a long moment, she said nothing and then the words began tumbling from her lips in disjointed spurts. "It was ... an accident. I didn't mean for ... I followed her ... I never ... I put her in the—"

Brock frowned. "Ssh. Don't say another word."

Ricki cast a harried glance over her shoulder at the prison guard in the booth in the corner of the room. He was engrossed in his phone, oblivious to their conversation. "Are you going to tell Palmer, or should I?"

Brock gave an adamant shake of his head. "No one's going to breathe a word of this to Palmer, or anyone else. I need you to promise me you won't say a thing. You're going to hire that lawyer this afternoon and get him on my case ASAP."

Ricki blinked back a torrent of tears. "Why are you trying to protect me?"

"Because what happened is my fault," he said urgently. "I can't blame you for thinking I was having an affair. I should have come clean from the outset."

"But you didn't kill her," Ricki whispered.

"Not directly, but my deception sealed her fate."

"And now I've sealed yours," Ricki mouthed back. "I'm going to find a way to fix this."

"Ricki," Brock pleaded. "This can't be fixed. Someone has to pay for it. We have to hire a lawyer and face the charges."

"I can confess." She lowered her voice. "I won't go to prison for long, not when they know what really happened. I only went to her apartment to tell her to stay away from you. It was an accident. She slipped and hit her head."

Brock gave a disconsolate sigh. "Do you really think a jury's going to believe that?"

Ricki shrugged. "I don't know. But whatever the end result, at least the truth will be out."

"The only person who'll believe it's the truth, is you. I have a better chance in court than you do. There's no evidence to connect me to Tay's murder."

"Please, Brock, I'm begging you to reconsider. If you go through with this, you run the risk of being convicted."

"I'll take that risk before I see you behind bars. I love you, Ricki."

"Time's up!" The prison guard called.

"I have to go," Ricki said, blowing him a kiss.

"Swear to me you'll say nothing about what we discussed," Brock urged.

"I can't make that promise," Ricki said, getting to her feet.

Brock reached out and gripped her by the wrist. "If you don't, I'll confess to murdering Tay."

41

The arraignment hearing was set for the following Monday. Brock would be forced to spend the weekend locked up contemplating his fate, while Ricki reflected on the choices she had made that had put him in this position. His threat to confess to Tay's murder had ended the debate on whether or not she should turn herself in, at least for now. She had little option but to wait and see how things played out at the hearing. In the meantime, she had retained a top-notch lawyer who was somewhat optimistic that Brock would be acquitted due to lack of any real evidence. The "somewhat" part scared Ricki. There was still the circumstantial evidence—Tay had essentially been blackmailing Brock, not to mention the fact that her body had been dumped in the lake next to the house where Brock was staying.

It was a huge red flag, but Brock hadn't been the only one with a good reason to want to dispose of Tay. Brock's lawyer, David, intended to hammer home the point that the police had done a shoddy job homing in on Brock as their prime suspect before sifting through all the facts. Both Jim and Alex had equally strong motives to want Tay dead. Ricki dreaded hearing David cast aspersions on her friends' husbands in front of a judge, but if it spared Brock from a false conviction, she would just have to deal with it. At least no one was looking at her, and they had no reason to. She could put all her focus and energy into saving Brock.

On Saturday, she spent the day going through their finances, trying to figure out how they were going to pay Brock's legal fees now that her stock option was on hold due to Alex draining the company's finances. She was shocked to discover that Brock had spent over eighty-thousand dollars on Tay in the few short weeks he'd known her. If the case went to trial, it would be a struggle for her to patch together the funds for bail. Hopefully, the judge wouldn't consider Brock much of a flight risk.

Monday morning rolled around, and before she knew it, she was settling into a bench several rows behind Brock and his high-priced lawyer, David Robinson. Ricki couldn't shake the guilt, knowing it should have been her sitting there, head hung low and handcuffed. Her stomach fluttered with a sense of impending dread. She had done all she could, for now. The rest was in the lawyer's hands. Glancing around, she noted the strategically posi-tioned armed sheriffs dotted around the courtroom, legs astride, their eyes roving over the occupants for any sign of unrest. The case had caught the attention of the media, and the courtroom was packed. Thanks to the catastrophizing news headlines plastered over the internet, the public was riveted by the idea of a father murdering the biological daughter he never knew existed until she began blackmailing him. It read like a seedy thriller—something Alex would write. Maybe this would be the story that would reignite his career.

"All rise," the court bailiff's voice boomed out, announcing the judge's entrance.

The proceedings got underway and the lawyers for the defense and prosecution stepped forward to introduce themselves.

"Good morning, your honor, David Robinson on behalf of Brock Wagner."

"Laura McKnight for the state of Nevada," a middle-aged woman with a neat bob and horn-rimmed glasses added.

The judge shuffled a few papers on his desk and cleared his throat to read the charges.

"Your honor," David spoke up. "I would like to waive a formal reading of the indictment and enter a plea of not guilty on my client's behalf."

"Duly noted and recorded," the judge replied. "I have reviewed the preliminary information and concluded there is enough evidence to bring this case to court. Motion to dismiss is denied. A trial date is set for July fifteenth. Does the state wish to be heard on bail?"

"Yes, your honor," the prosecution lawyer responded. "We would like to ask the court to consider a bond amount in the range of one-million dollars. Specifically, the defendant is charged with murder in the second degree and has access to a sizable amount of money and therefore must be considered a flight risk."

Ricki grimaced inwardly. The sizable amount of money had shrunk sizably over the last few days. After some deliberation, she had approached Maria for a loan, but with *XCellNourish* in a dire financial situation, her boss had been unable to help. Ivy had been sympathetic to her plight, but Jim had refused point blank to allow her to help out with *blood money* as he'd dubbed it.

Ricki clenched her fists in her lap as she listened to Brock's lawyer attest to his outstanding citizenship and lack of any previous record. "Your honor, in light of the aforementioned reasons, I would like to ask that a reasonable bond in the neighborhood of two-hundred-thousand dollars be set."

The judge frowned at the paperwork in front of him before removing his glasses and addressing the court. "Bond will be set in the amount of five-hundred-thousand dollars. The court will permit a cash surety with a ten-percent deposit." As he droned on, listing the conditions of bail, Ricki slowly let out the breath she had been holding. At the very least, Brock would be free while awaiting trial and not subjected to the indignities and dangers of prison life.

It was a step in the right direction, but a shaky one, at best. Something Brock had said was haunting her.

This can't be fixed. Someone has to pay for it.

42

Throughout the trial a few weeks later, Ricki sat directly behind Brock in the courtroom hanging on every exchange between the judge and the lawyers. She sifted constantly through their words, analyzing their tone for any clue as to how favorably things were going for Brock. David had gone from cautiously optimistic to uncertain as to the outcome. The state prosecutor had proven a worthy adversary and come out with guns blazing, depicting Brock as a man whose anger at Tay's unrelenting demands for money had simmered beneath the surface until he'd exploded in a fit of rage.

Ricki held her breath as she watched the judge enter the courtroom for the final time, his robes swaying like a curtain falling on the final act. Today would be either a day of deliverance or a day of doom. After the closing arguments, Brock's fate would be decided by a group of his peers. It was unthinkable that he was facing the possibility of life behind bars. In the weeks leading up to the trial, she had tried in vain to convince him that it would be better to let her turn herself in, but he held the unwavering view that he would be acquitted. Terrified that he would make good on his threat to confess to the murder, she had made the decision to wait out the court's verdict.

As the proceedings began, she zoned out, her eyes fixed on the back of Brock's head. It was hard to grasp the fact that she might not hold her husband again for a very long time. She couldn't allow herself to think like that. She had to think positive thoughts.

"Are you all right?" David whispered over his shoulder to her.

"Keeping it together," she answered, with a flicker of a smile.

David nodded, as he settled into the seat next to Brock. He adjusted his cuffs before leaning over and muttering something in Brock's ear. Ricki wished she knew what he was saying. Did he think Brock had a chance of walking out of here a free man, exonerated of all charges? Or was he preparing him for the possibility of an unfavorable verdict?

She shifted uneasily in her seat when the prosecutor got to her feet. "Members of the jury, this is a case about the choice this defendant made on June seventeenth to take the life of his biological daughter, Tay Nicholson." The prosecutor paused and scanned the courtroom for effect. "Why, you may ask, would a father murder his own daughter? Let me begin by telling you who Tay Nicholson was—she was a con artist, and a petty criminal who made her money by conducting drug deals, as well as funneling unsuspecting victims into an illegal loan shark scheme." She walked over to Brock and stood in front of him. "Tay was blackmailing the defendant, threatening to tell his wife about her existence, and guilting him into supplying her with a steady stream of money and gifts." She returned to pacing the courtroom floor in front of the jury box. "And just when he was beginning to understand what a conniving criminal his daughter was, he learned that she was also the unidentified woman in the bar with Emily O'Shaughnessy the night she died. Emily O'Shaughnessy, as you recall, was the only child of Ivy and Jim O'Shaughnessy, close friends of the Wagners." She gestured to Brock with a flick of her wrist. "To quote Mr. Wagner's own words, Emily was the daughter he never had. He idolized her. In fact, as his estate attorney testified in court this week, Mr. Wagner had designated Emily O'Shaughnessy as the beneficiary of his and his wife's estate. These facts alone give Mr. Wagner motive. He also had opportunity—he met with her alone at her apartment on multiple occasions. Ladies and gentlemen of the jury, Tay Nicholson's body was discovered in the water next to the dock at the lake house where Brock Wagner was staying the weekend she died. Hardly a coincidence. There can be no question that he is responsible for her death. I put it to you that he flew into a rage when he found out it was Tay who had spiked Emily's drink, and he lashed out at her. When he realized she was dead, he hastily tried to cover up his crime." The prosecutor paused and set her lips in a tight line as she pointed to the enlarged photograph of Tay's suitcase on display at the front of the court room. "This, ladies and gentlemen, is a suitcase bought and paid for by Brock Wagner—the very same suitcase he used to transport his daughter's body to Tamarack Creek Lake." She let out a long breath and surveyed the room once more. "Members of the jury, Brock Wagner had both motive and opportunity. You are now charged with reading the instructions from the court and deliberating. I trust your judgement and anticipate that you return a guilty verdict."

Ricki pressed her knees tightly together and cast a desperate glance in the jury's direction. Their faces were unreadable. A couple of them were busy jotting down notes. One of them stifled a yawn. Ricki glared at him. How dare he take his responsibility so lightly! Didn't he realize an innocent man's life hung in the balance? She flinched when David got to his feet and walked to the front of the courtroom. As always, he looked impeccable in his tailored suit, exuding unruffled confidence. She only hoped it would pan out in the result she so desperately needed. After adjusting his glasses, he inclined his head toward the judge. "May it please the court, members of the jury. Thank you all for your service this week, I know what an imposition this has been on your lives, and I appreciate your time and attention."

He wheeled around and pointed at Brock. "Let me begin by stating that Brock Wagner should not be sitting in that chair. He is an innocent man. This week, he sat in the witness box and patiently answered all of the prosecution's questions. He could have remained silent, but he has been extremely forthcoming. You just heard from the prosecution once again about the lifestyle Tay Nicholson lived, consorting with drug dealers and shady loan sharks, combing casinos at night for customers, a risky life where the odds of dying young are high. Any one of her competitors could have ordered a hit on her— perhaps even an ex-boyfriend or lover." He hesitated and squeezed his chin in a thoughtful manner. "In their haste to pinpoint a culprit, the police ignored the complete lack of evidence connecting Brock Wagner to Tay Nicholson's murder and failed to investigate her contacts in the seedy underworld she inhabited. I put it to you that Tay was killed as a result of a deal gone bad. In an attempt to cover up the hit, Tay's murderer dumped the suitcase containing her body into the lake at the Dalcerris' lake house—a location the loan shark she worked for was familiar with as he'd been collecting payments from Alex Dalcerri. Let me remind you, ladies and gentlemen, that this loan shark, Levi Hendrix, has an extensive criminal record and previously served time for armed robbery and drug trafficking."

He paused for effect, smoothing a hand down the length of his expensive tie as he surveyed the jurors. "Members of the jury, this is my last opportunity to talk to you about the gross injustice Brock Wagner is faced with, a man of impeccable standing in the community. Once again, I appreciate your time and attention given to this case. Please consider the appalling lack of evidence as you go back to deliberate. If you are wavering, unsettled, or unsatisfied, it is your duty as a juror to acquit on the grounds of reasonable doubt. We are asking for justice, and justice in this case is a verdict of not guilty."

With a final nod of thanks to the jury, David returned to his seat.

The judge peered out over the courtroom and cleared his throat. "Let's take a recess before we hear the state's summation and the jury begins deliberations."

A low murmuring filled the room as people began to file out. In the foyer, Ricki made a beeline for David. "How do you think it went?"

"As well as can be expected," he replied evenly.

"I'm worried about the fact that Emily was the main beneficiary in our will," Ricki said. "It proves how close we were to her. It might sway the jury to believe the prosecution's allegation that Brock lost control when he found out what Tay had done to Emily."

David's grave eyes met hers. "That's a minor point in the grand scheme of things. The fact that no other suspect has been named will work against us, but we've done all we can, at this point."

An icy tingle crept up Ricki's spine at his words. It sounded as though David had already resigned himself to a guilty verdict. All the money in the world couldn't save Brock if the jurors weren't convinced of his innocence. Would she live to regret her silence?

Back inside the courtroom, Ricki sat through the prosecution's rebuttal in a daze. She scarcely heard a word that was said, her attention firmly fixed on trying to interpret the impassive expressions on the jurors' faces. Every now and then, one of them glanced in her direction, and then quickly averted their gaze. Her fear mounted as the minutes ticked by. Surely, they would have tried to give her some kind of sign if they were on her side.

At last, the prosecutor took her seat, and the judge turned to face the jurors. "Members of the jury, you may now retire to the deliberation room. I have provided you with principles intended to guide you in reaching a fair verdict in this case. You are to exercise your judgement without passion or prejudice, but your verdict must be unanimous. You are dismissed."

An imminent sense of doom settled in Ricki's gut as she watched the jury get to their feet and file like executioners out of the courtroom, ignoring her silent plea for clemency.

43

The day ended with no verdict in sight. Before leaving the courtroom, David had briefed them on what to expect and how soon the jury was likely to reach a verdict, and what would happen once they did. At this point, it was a waiting game. The evening stretched on as the stilted conversation between Brock and Ricki dried up. She flipped aimlessly through the TV channels before switching it off and abandoning any attempt to fill the time like she would if this was any other ordinary day. She picked at the fuzzy cushion she was clutching in her lap. This wasn't any other day, and they weren't just any ordinary couple. They were waiting on a verdict that would determine whether they would be separated for the next few decades of their lives, or granted a whole new lease on life.

"I still don't know if we did the right thing," Ricki said in a small voice.

"We've been over this a thousand times," Brock replied, with an air of weary patience. "At least this way we get to roll the dice. If you had confessed, you would have gone to prison, no question. Dumping Tay's body in the lake was a catastrophic mistake. The only way it could possibly have been ruled an accident is if you'd called 911 the minute it happened."

Ricki gave a glum nod. There was a time and a place to do the right thing, and she had missed that window, by a long shot. She had convinced herself she could live with the guilt—it truly had been an accident, after all. But her subsequent actions continued to plague her conscience. Hesitating to call 911 was one thing, but omitting to calling them entirely was unforgivable. Brock had stood by her because he blamed himself for what happened. But if he was wrongfully convicted of Tay's murder, the guilt would be impossible for Ricki to live with. She had thought long and hard about what she would do if the jury returned a guilty verdict. She'd pictured turning herself into Palmer, confessing to everything, but would it change the outcome this late in the game? He might think she was just trying to spare her husband. Without any real evidence, the authorities might not even retry the case.

"If it's a guilty verdict, David said we can appeal it," Brock said, interrupting her thoughts. "It's not the end. We'll keep on fighting."

Ricki rubbed her fingers over her aching forehead. "An appeal will take years. In the meantime, you could be stuck behind bars for something you didn't do."

"Something I instigated," Brock reminded her.

The trill of his phone startled them. Their eyes locked, hope and dread merging in an unspoken exchange.

"It's David," Brock confirmed, sliding his finger across the screen to take the call. As though fearing the worst, he pressed the phone tight to his ear so Ricki wouldn't be able to hear.

She tossed aside the cushion she'd been picking at and perched on the edge of her seat, trying to listen in. They hadn't expected to hear from David again tonight. Surely the jury couldn't have returned a verdict already. Maybe there was something important David had forgotten to relay to them earlier.

She listened intently to Brock's one-sided conversation, desperate to glean any indication of what the call was about. "Yes ... I understand," Brock muttered. "Of course ... okay, see you then."

He ended the call abruptly and tossed the phone onto the couch. "The verdict's in. Tomorrow morning at nine."

Ricki swallowed the jagged lump in her throat. Her thoughts careened first in one direction and then another. It wasn't a good sign that the jury had deliberated for only a few hours. Didn't that usually mean a guilty verdict? She could see by the strained expression on Brock's face that he was wrestling with the same thoughts. "David said not to read anything into the timing. It means nothing. Absolutely nothing," he repeated like a mantra, as though trying to convince himself.

"I know that," Ricki replied. "It still doesn't make it any easier." She dropped her head into her hands and took a shaky breath. It was going to be another very long night.

As they walked into the courtroom together the following morning, Brock gave her shoulder a reassuring squeeze. Ricki took her seat and watched as her husband settled in next to David for the final time. The lawyer turned and gave her a tense smile that did little to reassure her. It had been difficult leaving the house with Brock this morning, knowing there was a possibility they wouldn't be returning together. She pushed the thought aside. There was also a chance this nightmare would end today—perhaps, in a matter of minutes. Her thoughts ping-ponged between hope and doom like a never-ending rally, stretching her nerves to breaking point. Goosebumps prickled along her arms, as she swallowed the acid dancing at the back of her throat. She wasn't sure she would be able to hold it together until the verdict was read. How would she react if it was unfavorable? Would she be tempted to jump up and confess in front of everyone—her friends and news crews included? She couldn't bear the thought of watching Brock being marched out of the courtroom in handcuffs, condemned to a life behind bars.

"Mr. Foreman, I understand the jury has reached a verdict in this case. Is that correct?" the judge asked, peering over his spectacles.

"Yes, your honor," a bald-headed man replied.

Ricki watched with bated breath as he handed the verdict to the bailiff who, in turn, presented it to the judge. She knew she wouldn't be able to tell anything from the judge's expression, which had remained frustratingly dispassionate during the course of the trial.

No doubt, decades of presiding over similar cases had groomed his mask of neutrality. He cleared his throat and looked up. "The verdict appears to be in the proper format. Mr. Wagner, will you please stand and face the jury."

Ricki quickly scanned the faces of the twelve jurors, each of whom stared studiously past her. Her heart sank, hope circling the drain, despite her best intentions to remain optimistic until the end. Everything appeared to be happening in slow motion around her as the clerk began to read. The sound was muted as though she were a fish in a tank watching the outside world, powerless to intervene—swimming in circles, like her spiraling thoughts. Just as she felt certain she was going to pass out, the clerk's voice broke through the fog in her brain. "The State of Nevada versus Brock Wagner, case number 2459381C-F. As to the charge of second-degree murder, we the jury find the defendant, Brock Samuel Wagner ... not guilty."

Ricki gasped, crumpling the tissue in her fist. Hot tears erupted and spilled down her cheeks. The remainder of the judge's comments were lost on her as he set about dismissing the jurors.

Brock jumped to his feet and wrapped his arms tightly around her. "Told you I'd be acquitted," he whispered, his breath hot in her ear. "It's over now."

She nodded, wiping her wet cheeks with the back of her hand. Her terrible secret was safe. Brock would never betray her.

44

TWO WEEKS LATER

"Hello there! Ricki Wagner, isn't it?" a raspy, female voice called out just as Ricki was climbing into her BMW to go grab lunch.

She spun around and blinked at the heavily made-up, rail-thin woman waving at her from across the parking lot. She furrowed her brow, trying to recall where she knew her from, but she couldn't place her. To the best of her knowledge, it wasn't anyone she knew through work. As the woman drew closer, Ricki observed her stained teeth and dark hair roots in bad need of a touchup. Instinctively, she gripped her purse a little tighter and cast a wary glance around, fearful it might be a scam.

"I'm sorry. Do I know you?" Ricki asked brusquely.

The woman tinkled a laugh entirely devoid of humor. "Not yet. But we'll have plenty of time to get to know each other better. I'm starving. How about we talk over lunch?"

Ricki frowned, her unease about the woman's intentions growing. Was she going to mug her? She might have an accomplice waiting in the wings, ready to pounce the minute Ricki let her guard down. "I'm afraid that won't be possible."

She reached for her car door and opened it, flinching when the woman pressed her painted talons into Ricki's wrist. "You really should find some time for me in your schedule." Her lips curved into a mocking smile. "It's the least you can do for Tay."

Ricki froze, blood leaching from her head. She turned and stared directly at the woman, her gaze traveling slowly over her features. A ball of dread mushroomed in her gut. Yes, there was a resemblance beneath the caked makeup—those high cheekbones, green eyes. This woman had been beautiful, once.

Her kohl-lined eyes narrowed in satisfaction. "Ah, so you recognize me."

"You must be ... are you Tay's mother?" Ricki choked out.

The woman nodded sharply. "Liv Nicholson. I'm sure Brock's told you all about me."

"I'm sorry for your loss," Ricki said, cautiously taking a step back from the woman. She couldn't help but notice the curious looks several of her employees were shooting her way as they headed out on their lunch breaks. She couldn't be seen conversing here with Tay's mother—it was too dangerous. She had to get rid of her, as quickly as possible, without making a scene. "Is that why you came here, to hear me say how sorry I am for your loss?" Ricki asked. "You weren't even in her life anymore."

"Is that what Brock told you?" Liv pressed her lips together and gave a dramatic shake of her head. "You can't trust anything that lying murderer says."

Ricki raised her chin defiantly. "Brock didn't kill your daughter. He was acquitted."

Liv lifted a thin shoulder and dropped it nonchalantly. "Oh, I know that. I followed the entire trial. I'm not interested in your condolences."

"Then, what do you want?" Ricki hissed.

Liv let out a scornful sigh. "I was under the impression that you were a highly intelligent woman, but here I am being forced to repeat myself only minutes into our conversation. I want you to take me to lunch."

Ricki wet her lips, debating what to do. She had no desire to strike up any kind of relationship with Tay's druggie mother, but if she didn't hear her out, she might prove hard to get rid of. Ricki had a feeling this was about money. Maybe she thought Brock owed her for all the years of child support she'd never asked for. Too little, too late. She wasn't entitled to a penny of their money now, and she wasn't going to get a penny. There was nothing to go after anyway. Between their legal fees and Tay's successful sabotage of *XCellNourish's* finances, Brock and she were perilously close to being broke.

"Get in," Ricki said, begrudgingly. She switched on the ignition and tapped the steering wheel impatiently while Liv fumbled with her seatbelt. "I don't have long. I have a conference call this afternoon I need to be back for."

Liv let out a long, nostalgic sigh as she ran her fingers admiringly over the leather seat. "It must be nice to be so important."

Ricki threw her an irritated look as she pulled out onto the road. "If this is about money, we don't have anything left to give you. We poured all our savings into Brock's defense."

Liv gave her a slit-eyed look. "Did he really do it?"

"Of course not!" Ricki snapped. "He was thrilled when he found out he had a daughter. If you hadn't kept that from him all these years, she might still be alive."

Liv gasped indignantly. "So it's *my* fault she was murdered? Is that what you're saying?"

"I'm saying her life might have been different, that's all," Ricki said, forcing herself to calm down. The last thing she wanted to do was antagonize the woman. There was no telling what she was capable of, especially if she was anything like her daughter.

Liv leaned back in her seat and stared through the windshield. "It's such a shame you had to waste all your money on Brock's defense. I mean, if the person who killed her had copped to it, you would have been spared that whole spectacle of a trial. It was all over the newspapers and everything. It must have been so humiliating, especially for a private person like you."

Ricki swallowed the hard lump that had suddenly formed in her throat. How did Liv know that about her? She and Tay must have stayed in touch after all. She kept her gaze fixed on the road ahead, relieved that the guilt in her eyes was shielded by her sunglasses. After Brock's acquittal, the police had turned their focus on the criminal circles Tay moved in searching for her killer. But Ricki still lived in constant fear that some little error she had made would lead them to her. Brock was growing increasingly concerned about her inability to sleep. Truth be told, she'd take the insomnia over the night terrors that descended when she did finally pass out from exhaustion.

Spotting a small diner tucked at the end of a strip mall, she signaled and swung left into the parking lot.

"*This* is where you're taking me?" Liv wailed, her voice trailing off like a deflated balloon. "I was hoping for something a little more upscale. You really are broke. I didn't picture you frequenting low class establishments like this."

Ricki ignored her as she clasped her purse and climbed out, eager to get away from prying eyes curious about the unlikely pairing. Inside the diner, she led the way to a small table in the back. Liv studied the plastic menu intently, agonizing over her choice until Ricki finally blurted out, "Look, I don't have all day. Pick something or I'll choose for you."

After the waitress had taken their orders, Ricki glowered across the table. "Why don't you start by explaining why you accosted me in the parking lot?"

Liv raised her tattooed brows. "That's a big word—a bit hostile, too. You're not on a conference call now. This is just a friendly lunch."

Ricki sighed in exasperation. "I don't have time for games. Why are we here?"

A small smile played on Liv's lips as she reached for her napkin and unfolded it. "I'd like for us to get to know one another better."

Ricki shook her head in disbelief. "What makes you think I want to get to know you? It's clear we have absolutely nothing in common."

Liv eyed her with a crafty grin. "We have something in common."

"What? Oh ... you mean ... Brock—" Ricki broke off, her cheeks reddening.

Liv threw back her head and cackled with laughter. She cast a quick glance around the diner and then leaned forward, lowering her voice. "You're not tracking, so let me help you out. I'm talking about how much we both hated Tay."

Ricki's lips parted in shock. Beneath the table, her knees began to shake. "I ... didn't even know her. Why would I hate her? Like I said, Brock was thrilled when he found out he had a daughter. He and I always wanted a child."

Liv cocked her head to one side. "And then, out of the blue, you were gifted one."

Their waitress appeared and plonked their plates of food in front of them. "Can I get you anything else?"

Ricki shook her head mutely, and the waitress shuffled off and began clearing a nearby table.

"I get why you hated her. It's understandable," Liv said, picking up the conversation where they'd left off. "You thought she was sleeping with your husband." She reached for a fry and dipped it in ketchup before sliding it into her mouth. "I hated her too. She was a tightwad with her money. Always judging me."

Ricki felt like someone was slowly filling her with sand, weighing her down until she was unable to move or think. Where was this going? Did Liv suspect she had something to do with Tay's death? No, she had no reason to. She was swinging in the dark. Ricki grimaced. No matter. She couldn't prove a thing. "I didn't hate your daughter," she said, through gritted teeth.

"That's not what the camera in her apartment shows." Liv smiled brightly across the table at Ricki as she took a bite of her burger.

A thousand tiny tendrils of fear began curling their way up Ricki's spine. "What camera? What are you talking about?"

Liv wiped her lips carefully on her napkin, her eyes boring into Ricki. "You think you're so smart, don't you? You think you're above the likes of me and Tay with your fancy education and your posh car. But you're only successful in your own little bubble. You're completely out of your depth in the world Tay moved in."

Ricki creased her brow. "You're talking in riddles."

"Let me spell it out for you," Liv said. "Tay's handler was a drug dealer as well as a loan shark. She conducted business for him on a regular basis. He had security cameras installed in her apartment that recorded everyone who came in and out—to monitor the trans-actions and make sure no one double-crossed him, including Tay." Liv reached into her purse and pulled out a small black recorder. She hit the play button and slid it across the table to Ricki. "This is a sampling of the audio. Tell me if you recognize this voice." She cocked an amused brow. "You might not want to put it on speaker."

Ricki reached for the recording device and pressed it to her ear.

"You're nothing but a freeloader ... women like you are takers, here today and gone tomorrow ... Tay? Are you .... are you all right? Tay, please wake up! Moan or something. Just let me know you're okay. Please, please, please, be all right."

Ricki's fingers shook as she set the device back down on the table. "What do you want?"

Liv pulled out a hot pink lip gloss and smeared it over her lips before smacking them together. "That's just the audio. You can imagine how incriminating the video is. I think we can come to an arrangement that's agreeable to both of us, a modest monthly stipend —I'm not as greedy as my daughter was. You keep up your end of the bargain, and I'll take your ugly little secret to the grave."

"You're blackmailing me?" Ricki whispered.

Liv dropped her lip gloss into her purse and shrugged. "Like I said, your type isn't cut out for this. You should have called 911 and faced the music."

"It was an accident," Ricki croaked.

"Try telling that to the judge." Liv let out an amused snort as she slung her purse over her shoulder. "Unlawful disposal of a human body is also a crime. Thanks for lunch, although next time, I pick the restaurant."

"Wait!" Ricki cried out. "You can't leave yet!"

"Why not? We'll have plenty of time to get to know each other better. Don't worry, your secret's safe with me. I never kill a golden goose." Liv blew her a kiss. "It was wonderful to finally meet Tay's stepmother. And to think we have so much in common, after all!"

Her lips twisted slowly into a mocking smile. "Tay was a real gift to both of us, wasn't she? The gift that keeps on giving."

EPILOGUE

"That should do it," Palmer said, with a nod of approval as he leaned over and switched off the recording device in the small interview room where Ricki had just concluded giving her formal statement.

"What happens now?" she asked, throwing a hesitant glance at her lawyer, Teresa. She'd been too humiliated to reach out to David to ask him to take on her case, not that she would have been able to afford him anyway. Teresa seemed competent enough to get her through the court process. At this point, she wasn't looking for a legal magician, she was ready to accept her sentence, whatever it amounted to.

"We'll need a copy of the video taken from Tay's apartment, along with the police and autopsy reports," Teresa said, sliding some paperwork across the desk to Palmer. "Everything's listed here. I take it a subpoena's been issued for the witness already—Liv Nicholson?"

Palmer rubbed his chin thoughtfully. "That won't be possible. Liv Nicholson overdosed last year."

Ricki's jaw slid open. "But ... I met with her. I just told you that."

Teresa shoved her glasses up her nose and fixed a stony gaze on Palmer. "If you're withholding information from my client—"

"Wait!" Ricki interrupted, laying a hand on Teresa's sleeve. "It's okay. I think I know what's going on." She took a deep breath and sat up straighter in her chair. "The woman I took to lunch was an undercover officer, wasn't she?"

Palmer interlaced his hands on the table in front of him. "We needed a confession."

Ricki wrinkled her brow. "Why? I don't understand. You had the camera footage from the apartment."

"No. We only have what you heard," Palmer explained. "The audio arrived in the mail anonymously—I suspect, courtesy of Levi Hendrix. We were beginning to investigate him and his business practices a little too closely for his liking. When we went back and swept Tay's apartment for cameras, they'd been removed. No doubt, there was a wealth of criminal activity on the hard drives."

Teresa cleared her throat. "Ricki, as your counsel, I strongly recommend you say nothing more until we've had a chance to converse."

Ricki ignored her, pressing on. "If you recognized my voice, why didn't you arrest me right away?"

Palmer raised his brows at Teresa, inviting her to take the question.

She tossed her head with an irritated air. "The court always looks more favorably on someone coming forward of their own volition."

"I was willing to give you twenty-four hours to turn yourself in," Palmer added. "I suspected all along Brock hadn't done it. As soon as I heard the recording, I knew why he never protested his innocence—even after CCTV footage put him at his engineering firm at the approximate time of Tay's death."

Ricki's lip quivered. "I didn't want him to go on trial, but he threatened to confess to Tay's murder if I came forward. He blamed himself for what happened. He didn't want to see me go to prison. I guess he will now."

Teresa tapped her pen impatiently on the desk. "I need some time alone with my client."

"Of course." Palmer got to his feet. "I'll leave you two to talk." He gave a curt nod and exited the room.

Ricki's phone beeped with an incoming text. She grimaced apologetically at Teresa as she fished around in her purse. "Let me just respond to this. It's probably my husband." She clicked on the message and opened it.

When will you be home? I picked up your favorite pasta for dinner.

Ricki tapped a fingernail on the screen, pondering her response for a moment before she messaged him back.

It's going to be a while. I've gone golfing.

A sad smile tugged at the corner of her lips. He would know right away where she was. In the weeks after his acquittal, *no more golfing* had become code between them for no more lies. She held her breath watching the three pulsing bubbles on the screen until Brock's response appeared.

Please tell me you're not where I think you are.

Squaring her shoulders, she began to type.

Right where I should be. Paying a debt. I love you.

~

A QUICK FAVOR

Dear Reader,

I hope you enjoyed reading *The Invitation* as much as I enjoyed writing it. Thank you for taking the time to check out my books and I would appreciate it from the bottom of my heart if you would leave a review, long or short, on Amazon as it makes a HUGE difference in helping new readers find the series. Thank you!

To be the first to hear about my upcoming book releases, sales, and fun give-aways, sign up for my newsletter at **www.normahinkens.com** and follow me on Twitter, Instagram and Facebook. Feel free to email me at norma@normahinkens.com with any feedback or comments. I LOVE hearing from readers. YOU are the reason I keep going through the tough times.

All my best,

Norma

WHAT TO READ NEXT

Ready for another thrilling read with shocking twists and a mind-blowing murder plot?

Check out my entire lineup of thrillers on Amazon or at www.normahinkens.com.

Do you enjoy reading across genres? I also write young adult science fiction and fantasy thrillers. You can find out more about those titles at **www.normahinkens.com.**

WHILE SHE SLEPT

While She Slept, the next book in the *Treacherous Trips Collection,* releases May 2023.

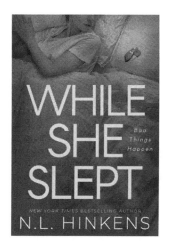

We have your husband. Question everything you know.
After losing her first husband to cancer, newlywed Abbey has found love again with dashing widower Declan Cafferty. On honeymoon in Ireland where Declan grew up, the idyllic start to their marriage is

everything Abbey hoped it would be. Until the morning Declan vanishes without a trace.

Plunged into a nightmarish investigation, Abbey becomes the prime suspect in his disappearance. But with no evidence to convict her, and no body to prove a crime has been committed, the Irish authorities have little choice but to let her return to the United States, while their missing person's case goes cold.

Just when Abbey has begun to put the pieces of her shattered life back together, she spots a woman she recognizes boarding a plane to San Francisco—a woman she was led to believe had died in a boating accident. It's Declan's first wife.

As Abbey begins to dig for answers, a treacherous web of lies quickly unravels. The truth has been hiding in plain sight.

Someone will stop at nothing to take everything.

- A heart-racing thriller with explosive plot twists and a jaw-dropping final reveal! -

∾

BIOGRAPHY

NYT and USA Today bestselling author Norma Hinkens writes twisty psychological suspense thrillers, as well as fast-paced science fiction and fantasy about spunky heroines and epic adventures in dangerous worlds. She's also a travel junkie, legend lover, and idea wrangler, in no particular order. She grew up in Ireland, land of storytelling and the original little green man.

Find out more about her books on her website.
www.normahinkens.com

Follow her on Facebook for funnies, giveaways, cool stuff & more!

BOOKS BY N. L. HINKENS

BROWSE THE ENTIRE CATALOG AT www.normahinkens.com/books

VILLAINOUS VACATIONS COLLECTION

- The Cabin Below
- You Will Never Leave
- Her Last Steps

DOMESTIC DECEPTIONS COLLECTION

- Never Tell Them
- I Know What You Did
- The Other Woman

PAYBACK PASTS COLLECTION

- The Class Reunion
- The Lies She Told
- Right Behind You

TREACHEROUS TRIPS COLLECTION

- Wrong Exit
- The Invitation
- While She Slept

NOVELLAS

- The Silent Surrogate

BOOKS BY NORMA HINKENS

I also write young adult science fiction and fantasy thrillers under Norma Hinkens.

www.normahinkens.com/books

THE UNDERGROUNDERS SERIES
POST-APOCALYPTIC

- Immurement
- Embattlement
- Judgement

THE EXPULSION PROJECT
SCIENCE FICTION

- Girl of Fire
- Girl of Stone
- Girl of Blood

THE KEEPERS CHRONICLES
EPIC FANTASY

- Opal of Light
- Onyx of Darkness
- Opus of Doom

FOLLOW NORMA

FOLLOW NORMA:

Sign up for her newsletter:
https://normahinkens.com/
Website:
https://normahinkens.com/books
Facebook:
https://www.facebook.com/NormaHinkensAuthor/
Twitter
https://twitter.com/NormaHinkens
Instagram
https://www.instagram.com/normahinkensauthor/
Pinterest:
https://www.pinterest.com/normahinkens/

Made in the USA
Monee, IL
04 August 2023

6e6977e1-8142-4596-be41-9340d7c54411R01